A Brain
in
Third Person

ISBN-13: 978-0-9972920-6-0
ISBN-10: 0-9972920-6-7

First printing: March 2017

Cover design by ThomasMax
Front cover photo by Robert Preston Ward

Published by:

ThomasMax Publishing
P.O. Box 250054
Atlanta, GA 30325
www.thomasmax.com

A Brain in Third Person

A. Shane Etter

ThomasMax

Your Publisher
For The 21st Century

ACKNOWLEDGMENTS

First I'd like to thank, from the bottom of my heart, my mentor, two-time Pulitzer nominee, Jedwin Smith. This is number three with your help and it keeps getting better. Thank you.

Jedwin introduced me to a great editor, Chuck Clark. Thank you for your magic, Chuck.

Thank you to the members of our ongoing Writer's Workshop. You challenge me and make me better. Although I don't always show it, I appreciate it.

Many thanks to Dr. Jacob Watters for letting me borrow your name and for help with all things medical and dead bodies.

To my sister, Amy Mills and my brother, CW5 U.S. Army, (Ret.), Kevin Etter, thank you for a lifetime of love and support.

Thanks to all my friends, old and new, writers and non-writers, who have supported me in words and actions. I will always be grateful.

And thank you to all of the great writers I read, for inspiring me and helping me, even if you don't know you're doing it.

Last, but not least, thank you Lee Clevenger of Thomas Max Publishing, for believing in "Brain."

Part 1
The First Seven

Chapter 1
The Crash

Spring 2014

Pennington Wentworth, II was on the way home to his 24th floor penthouse condo in the Buckhead section of Atlanta. It was on the north side of the modern high rise, with a view of the Dunwoody area of Atlanta and the north Georgia mountains miles beyond. It had been another frustrating Friday night out with his friends—men and women, the women very hot—but with whom he had no hope of ever having an intimate relationship. Women never seemed to look at him that way or think of him in those terms. The men, effeminate like himself.

He was five-foot-eight and weighed only one-hundred-thirty pounds. Lifeless and lank, mousy-brown hair did nothing more than cover his head, although he spent a small fortune for those less fortunate, getting it styled twice a month, at the most exclusive men's salon in Atlanta. Like himself, his stylist had thought he was gay the first time they met.

As for the night on the town with his friends, they'd had a pleasant time at a midtown comedy club, followed by dancing at the latest hotspot frequented by the beautiful people of Atlanta. On this night, Pennington's favorite comedian, Jo Koy, a Filipino who enjoyed making Asian women and families the butt of his jokes, had been on stage and Pennington's sides hurt and his mouth ached from laughing so hard. Pennington liked dancing with his women friends, especially slow dancing, which was the only physical contact he'd ever have with them. Part of the reason he and his friends went to these in-town nightspots was to keep from having to rub shoulders with people from outside the perimeter—OTPers as he and his friends liked to derisively refer to them. His crowd wouldn't have dreamed of venturing outside the perimeter, also known as Interstate 285 which circled the city. Lower status and definitely beneath them. Hopping on the connector from midtown back to Buckhead, it was only seconds before he was gaining on the red taillights, indicating a traffic jam of the sort a metropolitan area with a population of over seven million people would have.

He could afford any car he wanted but chose the solar-powered Toyota Prius due to his being environmentally conscious, and additionally, because the Prius allowed him to look down on those who weren't. Driving at a way-too-fast eighty-five—in the driving rain no less—he could sense that this time he would be unable to avoid an accident. At least the heavy torrent shielded him from seeing what happened next.

2:03 and 10 seconds A.M.

Jamming on the breaks as hard as he could, the Prius' tires locked up, the vehicle's control lost to skidding on the wet pavement. His blood pressure elevated immediately and he could feel beads of sweat pop out on his forehead.

2:03 and 11 seconds A.M.

Pennington could hear his heartbeat over the rev of the engine and the screech of the tires as the hydroplaning caused his speed to increase.

Gripping the steering wheel as hard as he could, he braced for impact, the pain in the muscles of his forearms like none he'd ever experienced due to having never lifted anything heavier than a Cosmopolitan glass. He regretted having never had sex with a woman.

2:03 and 12 seconds A.M.

He began to feel nauseous as he anticipated a deadly crash, feeling that he might be about to vomit, to ruin his tan-colored Versace slacks or his Hong Kong tailor-made custom white silk dress shirt, with the green-colored vomit—the remains of his expensive dinner from Kyma, the Greek Restaurant on Piedmont Street where other beautiful people like him and his group liked to dine in order to see and be seen. Typical for him, he had eaten nothing but vegetables, as he'd been a vegetarian since his high school years. He thought eating meat would make one aggressive and he had no desire to contribute to the killing of animals, besides not wanting protein to add any muscle to what he thought of as his metrosexual body.

2:03 and 13 seconds A.M.

He began to wish that he'd not spent most of his life partying and that his father, Pennington Wentworth, Sr., had instilled in him more of a work ethic. The Wentworth family scion might be more responsible had the patriarch not left him such a large inheritance.

2:03 and 14 seconds, A.M.

As he started to impact the Chevy Suburban—Oh God, this is it! He heard a woman's scream and then realized it was his own high-pitched voice. He had no recollection of the airbag's apparent malfunction.

2:03 and 15 seconds A.M.

The lightweight bumper and sheet metal front end of the Prius crumpled as it crashed into the much larger, and heavier people carrier. Reflexively raising his arms in front of his head, they hit the shattering windshield, ruining his one hundred dollar manicure and fracturing the bones in his fingers, hands, and forearms before his head eventually impacted the glass.

2:03 and 16 seconds A.M.

As the economical, politically–correct, environmentally-green vehicle started to fold like an accordion against the much larger SUV, the engine brackets broke free as designed, dropping its engine to the pavement so anyone in the car's compartment wouldn't be crushed by its own engine. The thought flashed in his head that he wished he hadn't been so politically correct and had bought a larger vehicle.

2:03 and 17 seconds A.M.

As the small car continued to fold, the driver's side leg–compartment blasted forward, shattering his feet, ankles and the fibula and larger tibia. If he managed to survive the crash it would be with a limp that would accompany him the rest of his life.

2:03 and 18 seconds A.M.

His light, summer weight sport coat offered him no protection. The steering wheel slammed into his scrawny chest, with a force, that if he survived it, would result in a massive bruise that would color even a much larger man's torso shades of black, blue and purple for months. A thought shot through his brain that maybe if he'd ever lifted weights he might have enough muscle and body mass to survive the impact.

2:03 and 19 seconds A.M.

His head finally made impact with the windshield. He was conscious for the crack of the bones of his frontal lobe. All thought and senses stopped. Darkness.

He was pinned unconscious in his expensive, new trash compactor.

Chapter 2
The Hospital

Due to the ubiquitous presence of cell phones and the widespread use of them medical personnel and law enforcement arrived simultaneously, almost before the chain reaction collision had ended. The windows of the tall buildings along the Highway 400 corridor reflected the dozens of flashing red and blue lights.

Near the tail end of the more than thirty car pileup, emergency personnel were able to get to Pennington quickly and place him among the first wave of casualties transported to Atlanta's Grady Memorial Hospital. Grady's emergency room was the most seasoned—some would call it overworked—in the city, due to the high number of accident and crime victims and illnesses common to one of the nation's largest cities.

The ER waiting area had the look of a MASH unit with all the bloody, broken people sitting in chairs, lying on the floor and if they were able, standing in the corners. The sounds were worse, with moaning, screaming and sobbing from patients in obvious pain. The resident smell of all hospitals—sewagy—from bodily waste, mixed with the aroma of industrial strength antiseptic cleansers.

Dr. Jason "Hawkeye" Pierce was nearing the end of his twenty-four hour shift when the first ambulances began to arrive. He'd been given the sobriquet, "Hawkeye", due to him having the same last name as the Alan Alda character, the surgeon/jokester, always ready with a quip, on the long-running, hit television show, "M*A*S*H". Ironic, because Dr. Pierce was not known for having a well-developed sense of humor. He didn't like the nickname, mostly because he didn't like being tied to the show with a theme song titled "Suicide is Painless." He took personal offense to it.

In fact he was known as being all business, and nurses and even other doctors tended to walk on eggshells around him for fear of incurring his wrath in the form of barked orders, scathing putdowns and a general air of "I'm-better-than-you". Sad, because he was. Respected for being an outstanding physician. It had been a fairly typical Friday night in the ER unit until then. Busy, but not abnormally so. The smell of burned hair and flesh from the many surgeries. A pair of gunshot victims, a half dozen car accident victims and an elderly man who'd fallen from a step ladder in his home and broken his pelvis. What he was doing on top of a step ladder at two o'clock in the morning was anyone's guess.

By 3:15 in the early pre-dawn, the ER staff began treatment on Pennington. Getting him stabilized and assessing the damage to his brain was the immediate task for Hawkeye. He was observed as being glassy-eyed, incoherent and in and out of consciousness. The ambulance personnel had placed a c-collar around his neck, to maintain stability and to prevent compromise to the phrenic nerve, which powered the lungs.

A CT scan called in by the on-call radiologist to Hawkeye revealed an epidural hematoma. With a large collection of blood over one hemisphere of the brain, Pennington would need immediate neurological surgery to evacuate the hemorrhage. Pennington's condition resulted in internal bleeding with blood in the stomach causing him to produce bloody vomit.

"Everyone on your toes. We've got to get him stable before Dr. Gable can do the surgery to stop the bleeding," Hawkeye shouted at everyone. "And even if we do, this one's going to have issues. He'll be guaranteed to have mental problems," he remarked under his breath to the senior nurse on duty. The frontal lobe where Pennington's fracture was was the area that controlled behavior, inhibitions and personality. The team proceeded to intubate the trachea to maintain respiration.

***

Pennington awoke to a vortex of activity in what appeared to be a hospital room. Unable to understand why he was there he concluded that he must be the patient.

"He's awake." Someone had noticed the first, slight movement of his left ring finger.

As he awoke, noticing the wires attached to his bruised and battered body, and due to a sore throat from having tubes inserted for two weeks, in a hoarse whisper asked, "What the fuck is happening here?" Even surprising himself, as he had never used that word before.

Everyone turned to look at the doctor on duty who calmly responded, "Mr. Wentworth, we're glad to have you back."

"What do you mean have me back? Where have I been? Where am I? " Pennington was taken aback by the array of tubes, wires, electrodes and electrical monitors reading his every bodily function and especially the Foley catheter draining his bladder via his penis and he was unable to remember when he was young enough to have worn a diaper.

Dr. Jacob Watters, tall, 6-4, a handsome, preppie-looking man in his mid-thirties, continued, "You're in Grady Memorial Hospital. And where have you been? Ahh…you've been out, for just about two weeks. But let me sit down and let's chat for a moment.

"Please excuse us," he said to the cadre of medical personnel that was more than happy to oblige him. After everyone had departed Dr. Watters sat down in the cheap vinyl-covered chair in which many family members had sat, worried and slept while visiting their loved ones.

"I'm Dr. Watters. Your internist while you're in Grady. Tell me, Mr. Wentworth. What do you remember?"

"About why I'm here?"

"That's right."

Do I know why I'm here? What a stupid fucking question. "Not a goddamn thing." Something about the doctor just annoyed the hell out of Pennington and he would've liked to stretch the stethoscope he wore, around his goddamn neck and choke the shit out of him. He didn't know where those malicious thoughts were coming from. And he had no idea why he was using such profanity. He'd never had an aggressive fiber in his being. He literally wouldn't have hurt a fly, shooing them outside instead of killing them. All he knew was that a rage, caused by this doctor, was building up inside of him and he didn't know what to do about it. He needed an outlet for that rage.

Dr. Watters was not accustomed to patients behaving in this manner. Most patients understood that doctors were trying to help them, to heal them, and they tended to be respectful if for no other reason than for fear of causing the medical personnel to resent them and not do their best in caring for them.

"I have a novel idea. Why don't *you* tell *me* why I'm here." Pennington said to Dr. Watters.

"You were in a 30-car pileup on the connector in Buckhead, ah, let's see, two weeks ago today. Your skull was fractured, and you suffered a traumatic brain injury. A TBI is the term we use." He continued, "We—actually a neurosurgeon—performed surgery on you to evacuate the blood.

"Surgery? What? Brain surgery? Who gave you permission?"

"Our staff did their research and they determined you had no immediate family, so in cases like yours we have implied consent if the patient's life is at risk. We also went to a local judge and he made himself your custodian, to make decisions on long term care."

"Well shit!" This was going from bad to worse. A judge acting as his custodian. He didn't know what it was he didn't like about it but he innately knew that he didn't want anyone in law enforcement or the courts of law that near to him.

"So what happens now? What's my prognosis?" Pennington was afraid for his health. He'd been one of those rare men, the kind who actually saw a doctor regularly. And he and his internist had a close personal friendship.

"Well," he said, searching for the gentlest, but most straight forward words, "you had a frontal lobe injury. The frontal lobe is the part of the brain that controls one's personality, actions and inhibitions. All the decision making. With the type injury you had, with the severity of it, you can expect personality change, change in your likes, the food you eat, music you listen to, people you hang out with, everything about you could be different."

Pennington thought. *That must explain why this asshole pisses me off so and why I feel like I want to strangle him. And the language I'm using.*

But something highly unusual is occurring."

"Tell me. What is it? What else is wrong?"

"Calm down, Mr. Wentworth. It appears all of your injuries, including your fractured skull, are healing much faster than normal. You seem to be weeks ahead of schedule. It's almost like something else has taken over and is bringing you back quicker than normal."

"So what do I do?"

"We can release you if you have anyone you can stay with. We advise against anyone with this type of injury to be by themselves. And you will need to return for outpatient therapy, physical, occupational and speech, and I would recommend psychological therapy to help you deal with the mental and emotional changes I expect you'll be seeing."

"Well let's do it then, get me out of here. I'll be ready to go in five."

"Not so fast. I'll send a nurse in to help you get dressed."

"Well get to it, hotshot. I'm ready to get out of this joint."

Dr. Watters thought to himself, *the most arrogant jerk I've ever met.*

Chapter 3
The Change

The nurse Dr. Watters summoned entered and Pennington asked her, actually he ordered her, to help him find his latest generation iPhone. He was also worried about finding his Patek Philippe Celestial watch and his Louis Vuitton doeskin wallet. After she retrieved all three from a dresser drawer for him, Pennington made sure his American Express Black card was still in the wallet and then called his friend, Ashley Denson, to see if she could pick him up.

"I guess you know I'm in this shit-hole."

"What?" She was stunned to hear Pennington use that kind of language.

"Grady, Grady Memorial."

"Of course I know."

"Well, pick me up."

"Don't you mean, can I pick you up?"

"Yeah, whatev'. When can you be here?"

"After work, about 5:30? And that's only if I leave right on time.

"Shit, you can't get here before then?"

Shocked again, she ignored his language. "Unlike you Pennington, some of us have to work."

"Just get here as soon as you can. And I might need to crash at your place. The asshole doctor says I can't stay by myself."

That will never happen. It's like he's another person, he's completely different. I don't even know who he is. Pennington's always been so proper, and considerate of other people, and never used foul language.

The Friday afternoon rush hour traffic from Ashley's midtown real estate office where she worked selling Atlanta's high-end housing market, was typical. Unbearable. She hoped Pennington would be in a better mood and more like himself when she saw him in person. She thought that she should give him a break. She knew he'd been through a lot. A severe head injury and a two-week stay in a hospital would unnerve anyone.

Ashley entered his room at 5:45 and was greeted with, "Fuck, you're fifteen minutes late." He had been monitoring the red neon digital clock since before 5:30, watching the numbers tick by painfully slowly while becoming more enraged by the minute.

"Pennington, darling, I said I'd be here *about* 5:30. Traffic was atrocious."

"Yeah, yeah, just get my stuff—and get the nurse. She said she'd bring a wheelchair.

"Are you hungry, dear, would you like a salad, or sushi, or…"

"Rabbit food or smelly raw fish? I want a burger." His rage continuing to build, and now Ashley was in his sights. "The biggest goddamn burger we can find."

"But Pennington, dear, you don't do red meat."

"Yeah, well, a man can change, can't he?"

The nurse arrived and delivered Pennington to the hospital's rear entrance that served the visitor parking lot. Outside the stench from the row of dumpsters filled with rotting food and hospital waste was sickening. Ashley's small Infiniti she used for taxiing clients to see Atlanta's toniest properties, was a few parking spots away. They helped Pennington into the front passenger seat and got him settled.

Running her fingers through her own shoulder-length auburn tresses, she said, "And do you want to stop by your stylist? I'd suggest a haircut and a shave. Two weeks in the hospital has left you a wee bit ragged."

"Nah, I'm thinking of letting my hair grow out, and growing a goatee, or maybe even a full beard."

"What's wrong with you? This isn't the Pennington that I know."

Pennington balled up his fist and punched the wood grain dashboard of the small luxury car.

"That's just it, dammit. I don't know what's wrong with me. It's like someone else, or something else, is in control of my body. My brain just doesn't seem like mine anymore. It and I are at odds. It seems like since I woke up my brain and I disagree on everything."

"Well darling, I hope you will make an appointment to see someone, talk to a professional about it."

"Yeah, that's the same thing that asshole doctor said. But I don't want any goddamn shrink prying around in my head, even if my brain is acting a little different. The last thing I want is to get my head shrunk. Let's just stop talking about it and get me a goddamn burger."

"But Pennington, dear, listen to you. You aren't acting a *little* different. It's like you're a totally different person. You don't use language like this. You don't DO long hair. You don't DO red meat. I'm worried about you."

"Thank you for being concerned. If I think about it too much I'll get worried too.

"Good. Maybe you're not too far gone, then, dear."

'So let's talk about something else."

Chapter 4
The New Look

Waking up in Ashley's perimeter north apartment felt little different to Pennington than his own Buckhead condo. The north facing view was similar. He could see the beautiful north Georgia mountains he so loved. Not that he'd ever consider climbing or even hiking in them. He didn't exercise and didn't like to sweat. The thing Ashley liked most about her apartment was the short walk to Perimeter Mall and its exclusive department stores and shops and nearby dining and wine-bars. The Nordstrom Rack outlet store was her favorite shopping destination and she loved Alon's Bakery, a European style wine-bar, coffee shop and bakery with the best, to-die-for baked goods. She loved its international flavor. There was always a large number of Asians enjoying its breads and pastries and others looking to bring back memories of visits to or lives lived in Europe. Another favorite was Café Intermezzo, another combination wine-bar and coffee shop with the finest in European-style desserts. It was her favorite late night spot for a glass of wine or a cup of flavored latte.

Ashley was working on this Saturday, real estate's busiest day of the week, especially during the beautiful Atlanta spring weather. Azaleas of various colors were in bloom throughout the city. Beautiful, but the blooms of the various flowers combining with all of the pine trees wreaked havoc on one's sinuses during the early spring allergy season.

She'd already put fresh Starbuck's beans through the grinder before leaving and Pennington helped himself to a cup. But for the first time since he'd started drinking coffee, he eschewed French vanilla creamer, or a sweet macchiato, to have the strong dark roast black with a German rock sugar he found in a canister on the counter.

He poured a second mug and carried it with him to the bathroom. He knew that if he had to stay with Ashley for more than a couple of days he'd need to pick up some of his personal care items, his Sonicare dental appliance, his Waterpik and his hair and skincare products, Looking in the mirror before shaving he cupped both sides of his face in his hands and decided he liked the look of the dark stubble. He thought it made him look, dare he say it, manly–even rugged. So that was it. He was going with the rougher-looking, preppie no-shave-weekend beard length and longer-haired look. Saturdays were when he usually got his hair cut and styled, but not today. He figured he'd save that two-hundred dollars, not that he really cared considering his wealth, but it wouldn't hurt to use that money for something else…like alcohol, and besides, he didn't think he could stand the sight of that effeminate bastard who cut his hair anyway. That made him laugh because he knew that's the way most people thought of him.

***

Upon returning from her day of chauffeuring clients to view available homes and estates, Ashley offered to let Pennington accompany her and a friend, Cindy, a pretty Asian woman of Vietnamese descent, to one of their favorite dance spots.

"Sounds good." Pennington was ready for a distraction from the previous two week's hospital stay and the doctor's appointments he anticipated lay ahead.

"I need to run by the mall, pick out something to wear tonight and then tomorrow you can take me to my place to pick up some things I need."

"Okay dear. We can go to Nordstrom's, and I'll be happy to run you to your apartment tomorrow."

***

Dressed in his new Gucci sky-blue silk and wool sport coat, light-colored Armani slacks, blue Versace open-collared dress shirt and Prada shoes, Pennington felt good about the way he looked—and he especially liked his new facial hair, a two-week-old growth, longer than a stubble—but not a full beard—to go with his new, slightly longer hair. The fragrance he wore was Spicebomb by Viktor & Rolf. *We'll see what the ladies think now.*

Sage, a classy bar and dance club where mostly youngish-middle aged, stylishly dressed singles and couples hung out, listening sometimes to live music and other times dancing to the latest tracks playing on their expensive sound system, was not one of Pennington's regular haunts, but he liked the vibe it gave off when he entered. Passing by the bar on the way to the romantic dimly-lit dining room, Penny noticed the bar was topped with a bright blue glass lighted from below, giving everyone and everything in that area a neon blue tint.

Grabbing a table in the back, Ashley and Pennington waited for Cindy. They both felt the tension of wondering when someone would say, or do, something that would set Pennington off. It didn't take long.

After a few minutes of listening to the latest dance beats, the music of Fun, Pink, Farrell, and others, he'd had enough. "I can't stand this bullshit. They need to play some rock and roll!" Pennington shouted as he stood up.

"Who do I talk to about the music in this dive?" he directed at no one in particular.

"Pennington, don't," Ashley said, reaching for him.

"What do you mean don't? Don't what? I'm paying fifteen fucking dollars for watered down scotch. The least they could do is play some music I want to hear."

Upon hearing the ruckus, the manager came over to find out the cause of the commotion, which served only to make Pennington even more irate. The man was a stuffed shirt like his preferred clientele.

"What seems to be the problem, sir?"

"I'll tell you what the god damn problem is. The fucking music sucks. I want to hear some rock and roll."

"Sir, Sage is an upscale, high end dance club," he said haughtily, "We don't play rock and roll."

"Well, maybe you ought to try it and you wouldn't have so many goddamn stuffed shirts in here." Pennington continued to get louder. "Of course, you probably like stuffed shirts."

The insult appeared to go over the manager's head, that, or he was being too courteous to respond. "Sir if you don't calm down I'll be forced to call the police."

Threats to call law enforcement seemed to calm him down to a degree, causing him to relax a bit.

"All right, okay. I don't want any trouble," he said, straightening his sport coat lapels and smoothing his hair. "Except my fucking head hurts. I've got a cracked skull, you know."

"What are you drinking, sir? Your next one is on me."

"That's more like it. Eighteen-year-old Macallan." He'd been drinking twelve-year-old but if the manager was going to make him an offer of free booze he was going to take advantage of the man's generosity.

"I'll send one right over, sir."

Soon after settling down again, Ashley's friend, Cindy, arrived. Ashley and Cindy air-kissed each other European-style, on both cheeks.

"Cindy, I want you to meet my friend, Pennington Wentworth."

"Pennington, this is Cindy Nguyen."

"It's lovely to meet you, Pennington."

"Likewise." He said it more like a growl than a greeting. His brain injury caused him to sound pissed off even when he wasn't or didn't want to be.

After asking Ashley what she was having, Cindy ordered the same thing and the server brought her a glass of the house chardonnay, a mid-priced Kendall-Jackson.

Pennington and Ashley finished their first drinks about the same time and he said, "Let's hit the floor."

The dance floor was made from the same blue glass as the bar and also illuminated from below making all the dancers look like a different kind of Blue Man Group. He would've preferred to slow dance with her but after being out of commission for awhile even fast dancing would be better than nothing. He had to be careful since even though the doctor said his injuries were healing abnormally fast, his injured legs were still sore from the accident. The next tune was *We Are Young*, by Fun.

Said Ashley, "I love this song."

Taking her by the hand, Pennington said, "Yeah, let's do it."

As he tried out some of his moves, even though he had to scale them back a bit due to his injuries, he thought, *Yep, the chicks are digging what they see.*

And some of the guys were checking him out as well. But not in a gentlemanly way. Men just naturally didn't like Pennington in some cases, due to his effeminate looks and mannerisms, and that he was often with some of the hottest women. What they didn't know was the women were just friends and those men could still approach the women he was with. And that's what one did. Only this time Pennington didn't take it lying down.

As Ashley and Pennington returned to their booth, one of the men who'd been watching them on the dance floor approached them asking Ashley if she'd like to dance.

"Hey buddy, can't you see she's with somebody. Or are you blind?"

"Hey it's okay." He held his hands shoulder high, palms facing forward, in a be-cool, gesture. "It just didn't seem like you were *together*."

"Well, buzz off, asshole. We are."

"Yeah, I'm the asshole. Look who's talking."

He walked away and Ashley said, "Well, Pennington, darling, we're not really together. And that's happened before and it's never seemed to bother you."

"Well, it bothered me this time and people are going to start showing me some goddamn respect."

Cindy sat quietly, embarrassed, not knowing what to think. Ashley had told her about her friend, Pennington, before, but she'd never mentioned him being like this. Boorish, crude and unable to mind his manners in polite society.

After a moment of tense silence, Pennington said, "I'm going outside for a smoke." Since Ashley had never known him to smoke, she suspected it had to be another one of the unusual affectations he was experiencing.

Park Place, where Sage was located, had an open courtyard in the center, around which all the cafes, bars and shops surrounded. A pleasant, larger than one acre setting with park benches nestled among trees, blooming shrubs and the newly greening lawn in the nascent Atlanta spring.

He settled into a small sitting area screened from view by large shrubs. He could sit unnoticed, watching as people trickled out of Sage making their way to other clubs late on a Saturday night, that was ticking forward to the dawning Sunday morning.

His attention was drawn to the asshole who'd asked Ashley to dance, leaving alone, making his way to the rear parking lot.

Unbeknownst to him, the sidewalk on which he walked would take him past Pennington's position, hidden though he was from view. A minute or more from the guy's approach, a foot-and-a-half length of two-by-four Pennington noticed nailed loosely to a tree, the remains of a kid's treehouse from a bygone era, long before Park Place was built, when this part of Atlanta was rural, wooded, countryside, gave him an idea. A delicious, mean-spirited, idea. Although he knew he was brain-damaged he couldn't believe that that alone was causing his malicious thoughts. He felt like someone else, or something else was controlling his thoughts and actions.

Pennington pulled out the Brunello Cucinelli pocket square from his sport coat breast pocket and wrapping it around his hand to prevent the possibility of a transfer of fingerprints, silently stretched out the length of the bench to pull the board from the tree. Although, as weak as he was from his hospital stay and a lifetime of almost no physical exertion, it took more strength than he'd thought himself capable. He was pleased with himself when after a struggle, he managed to wriggle it free. He hoped his plan wouldn't ruin the one-hundred-twenty-five dollar handkerchief. Wealthy as he was, it really didn't matter to him much, but his love for the finer things in life would cause it to make him a little sick.

As the asshole neared, Pennington timed his exit from his concealed position so that he would fall quietly in step behind him, a little more than an arm's length to the rear.

From his position right behind, Pennington said, "Hey asshole."

And as the unsuspecting victim began to turn around, although Pennington swung like a girl, he brandished the length of board with both hands and with all his might, connected at the perfect position for maximum impact to the left rear side of his adversary's head. Pennington felt the asshole's skull crushing under the aged wood of the ladder rung and heard and felt the crunch of the bones breaking. He loved the visual of the asshole's still form falling like a body without bones, collapsing to the sidewalk.

Pennington felt momentary glee at the prospect of this asshole suffering the same fate, having the same injury, a fractured skull, as he had.

Since his act was unplanned it occurred to him that *Discretion is the Better Part of Valor*, and he decided he should get as far away from there as possible and started the less than fifteen minute walk back to Ashley's high-rise. He was glad his brain was functioning well enough to have the forethought to ask her for a key. As he walked he heard sirens and saw blue lights moving in the direction of the club.

Passing a block of low rent buildings, a neon sign caught his eye: "The Bad Penny Pawn Shop." He'd thought for some time that if he hadn't been saddled with such a proper British-sounding name at birth, his life might have turned out differently—Bad Penny—that would be a helluva name. People would respect someone called Bad Penny. And right then and there, he decided that Bad Penny would be his nickname.

When Ashley returned home about 2 a.m., Pennington was watching a scary-as-shit-movie, *Them,* on her widescreen television. The sound of her keys in the lock, startled him. He wrote it off to the frightening movie at the late hour and to his being on edge from his little misdeed, as he characterized it.

"What happened to you? Where'd you go?"

Playing it cool, he said, "What do you mean?"

"When you left."

"Well, like I told you, I went out for a smoke, then decided I was tired of dealing with assholes for one night, so I came back here."

"Really?"

"I shit you not."

"Well, you missed all of the drama."

"What do you mean?"

"Some guy, I didn't see who it was, got mugged in the courtyard."

You're shittin' me."

"Pennington, darling, you know I don't do that."

"Well, hot damn. I'm sorry I missed it."

"Pennington! From what I heard, he got hit on the head with something heavy, and has a fractured skull. They don't know if he'll live."

"Just kidding. Bad joke. I'm sorry for his misfortune."

"All right then."

"You should probably be more careful, going to questionable places like that. I couldn't bear it if something happened to you."

"You're so sweet. That's the Pennington I remember.

"By the by, I need you to drive me to my condo in the morning."

"To pick up some of your clothes?"

"No, I'm thinking about going home."

"Pennington, you can't. The doctor said…"

Interrupting Ashley, Pennington said, "I don't care what that son-of-a-bitch said. I can't keep imposing on you."

"Well, you have to do what you have to do, but I wish you'd think about it before you decide."

***

Ashley drove Pennington to his apartment on her way to the office for Sunday afternoon appointments. They dropped by Alon's for a healthy, European-style breakfast; They each ordered a Mediterranean omelet, full of veggies, with breakfast potatoes and shared a carafe of coffee. She also picked out a selection of fresh-baked pastries to share with her clients. Pennington seemed happier and more like himself, which she was glad to see. With a good night's sleep and a new day, maybe he was turning the corner.

His apartment was on the way to her office and after saying good-bye to Ashley, Pennington took the elevator to the 24th floor, enjoying the private time to be alone in his thoughts. He regretted hitting the asshole with the board, even if he was an asshole. He hoped his normal, non-violent, pacifist self would soon return. He'd have to call his personal physician Monday morning, make an appointment, find out what the doc thought, his recommendations, for a plan of treatment; of course he couldn't tell the doc about what he'd done.

Pennington entered his condo, amazed as always at the view of the mountains from his living room floor-to-ceiling window. It wasn't just the view, or the modern conveniences however, his home offered that he enjoyed, but also the diversity of high-rise life—the many middle easterners, Asians, African Americans and caucasians of varying ages and backgrounds that he enjoyed. He also enjoyed seeing the various dogs that neighbors walked. And thought he might like to get a dog; a big, tough Rottweiler or German Shepard. Lost in the view, but realizing he wanted a drink, he walked over to the seventeenth century French armoire for which he'd paid over seventeen thousand dollars and used as a bar and studied his bottle selection, and realized all he had were high-end wines—cabs, Bordeaux's and burgundies, and chards. The last time he'd been to Napa Valley he'd shipped back five cases of wine, one from each winery he'd visited. Not a drop of whiskey or a beer in the place. Since like the doctor at Grady had predicted, his tastes seemed to be changing with this new brain of his, it appeared a trip to the liquor store was on the agenda. And his preppy wardrobe wouldn't cut it anymore. He needed some basic jeans, maybe in black, some t-shirts and with the warmer summer months coming, maybe even a couple of wife beaters. And some boots.

But maybe he was getting carried away. He hated to throw out his fine clothes and—who knew—maybe his brain change wasn't permanent.

Chapter 5
Alternative Treatment

Pennington called Dr. Spenser's office and because he was a long-time patient and friend of the doctor's, the receptionist said they could accommodate him with an appointment that afternoon. Though he had to borrow a car from a friend before he could go anywhere. He'd have to buy a new one since his was totaled in the accident.

***

Dr. Spenser entered the examination room where he waited.

"So, how're you feeling, Pennington?"

"My god damn head hurts, Doc. My skull cracked open like a ripe cantaloupe."

"That's what I understand. We'll need to get you setup for physical and occupational therapy and probably speech as well."

"Damn, isn't there anything else we can do instead of all that?"

"Well, it depends on how open-minded you are."

"What do you mean?"

"Alternative medicine. The Chinese have had success treating brain injuries with acupuncture for hundreds of years."

"And I could do that instead of all those other treatments?"

"Possibly, but from what I hear it can be pretty painful—and insurance may or may not cover it."

"Well I'm willing to try anything. Can you recommend an acupuncturist?"

"No, we didn't go to the same schools, and don't run in the same circles, but I'd bet if you looked around the Asian community in Doraville you'd be able to find a reputable one."

He thanked Dr. Spenser and after leaving rode up to Doraville in search of acupuncturists. Only thirty minutes up I-85 from the doc's midtown office, Doraville was the center of greater Atlanta's Asian community. Made up of Korean restaurants, Asian banks and Chinese massage studios, the anchor of the neighborhood was the enormous Buford Highway Farmers Market, known by locals as the Asian market, with large quantities of whole fresh fish, breads of various persuasions and the most amazing array of international produce one has ever seen. And the customers were a diverse mix of Asians,

Latinos, African Americans, Jewish people and whites who desired high quality, inexpensive, ethnic foods. Pennington had discovered it several years previously when, on a New Year's Day with nothing else to do since he didn't watch football, went with a male friend, since out-of-the-closet, who introduced him to all the delights of the store.

A nearby building caught his eye, a small white-painted house, mostly likely built in the 1940's, surrounded by a white picket fence. The hand-painted sign hanging above the front porch read, "Dr. Wu, Acupuncturist and herbal medicine. Pulling over and getting out his iPad, he entered the name so he could Google it.

Even though he wouldn't have dreamed of doing it before his head injury, he surfed the internet while driving. Pennington Googled Dr. Wu. Located a website and found out Dr. Wu was female and had been practicing acupuncture for more than 45 years. He thought to himself, *that's good, because I wouldn't want to be her first patient.* He cracked himself up sometimes. Switching to his cell phone, he called her office and the man who answered the phone was able to arrange an appointment for a consultation and first treatment for the following morning.

***

A few minutes after arriving home his cellphone rang and it was the building's concierge.

"There are a couple of ah…gentlemen here to see you, Mr. Wentworth."

"Well, who are they?"

"They asked me not to say who they are."

"Then fuck 'em. Send 'em packing."

"I suggest that you should see these gentleman, sir." Peterman's formality was obvious in every word he uttered.

"Well I don't care what you suggest."

"Sir, trust me. You should see them."

"Okay—maybe I won the Goddamn Publisher's Clearinghouse. Send them up," he said chuckling.

Peterman keyed the elevator for the detectives and as it opened *Sympathy For The Devil* played on the piped in music.

Ramsey, annoyed, said, "There's something inherently wrong with a soft-rock instrumental version of Sympathy For The Devil."

Townsend agreed. "You know, brothers hardly even listen to the Stones, but I agree with you completely. You want a breath mint?" he asked Nick as he popped a Mentos.

"No thanks.

The doorbell chimed, and Pennington opened the door and could tell immediately they weren't from Publisher's Clearing House although the shields they produced were made of gold. The African-American one said "I'm Detective Anthony Townsend. My partner— Detective Nick Ramsey." Ramsey nodded. It was funny to Pennington how it seemed that detective partners always followed the Hollywood script of how a director thought they should look. Townsend was ebony, tall, angular, about Pennington's age and dressed like a GQ model. Ramsey was ten years older and dressed like Columbo in the old television series, looking like his suit had been pulled out of a camel's ass, rumpled and threadbare.

"This must be about that guy that was hurt Saturday night at Park Place."

"You know about that." It was a statement, not a question.

"Only what my friend told me. I left before it happened."

"His name *was* Matthews, John Matthews. It's no longer an assault. It's a homicide." Townsend oozed gravitas from his pores.

"Good God almighty, in that neighborhood. That's one of Atlanta's best areas."

"Crime knows no neighborhoods," Ramsey said.

Pennington chuckled to himself. He thought the scene sounded like it was taken from an old *Dragnet* episode, the 60's era television police drama.

"Getting to the point, we need to ask you a few questions," said Townsend.

"By all means." Pennington said, going back to his normal persona, weak, effeminate and syrupy sweet. "Why don't we retire to the living room? Would you gentlemen like a nice cup of hot tea? It is almost teatime."

"None for me. Thanks." Ramsey was afraid he was beginning to have prostrate problems and didn't want to risk having to go to the bathroom in this guy's apartment.

"Me neither," Townsend agreed.

"If you all don't mind I'll have some. This has me so upset I could just cry."

"Help yourself. What we have won't take long." Ramsey was already having doubts that this small, effete guy could have had anything to do with it.

After putting on some water to heat, Pennington returned to the living room carrying an assortment of cookies on a Gail Pittman platter from his matching collection of dishes, bowls and serving pieces. He set the platter of cookies on the sofa between the detectives and said, "Please, won't you have some." Then he sat down in a high-backed Queen Anne-style chair across from the sofa. The living room of the condo was filled with pieces, either antiques or expensive reproductions representative of the 1700's Queen Anne era. The walls covered with artwork, both local Atlanta artists and nationally recognized, the highlight of his collection, a Peter Max original for which he paid $75,000. And since he won it at a charity auction, with it he earned the privilege of meeting Peter. And they'd maintained an email relationship that he liked to refer to as a friendship, since.

"So, I'd be honored to help you gentlemen if I'm able. How do we start?"

After examining a cookie, Ramsey placed his chewed gum in an empty candy dish and taking the cookie, popped it in his mouth, nodded his approval, and took the lead. "What time did you leave Sage?".

"Well let's see. When I walked outside it was just to have a smoke, so noticing the time wasn't that important to me, but if I recall, it was about 11:30."

"So once outside you decided to leave?" Ramsey.

"Pretty much."

"And where did you go?"

"I walked back to my friend's apartment."

"That would be Miss Denson." It wasn't a question. Ramsey.

"Yes."

"You'd had a confrontation with the deceased earlier?" Ramsey.

"Oh my goodness, that's who it was?"

"You didn't know?" Townsend thought that odd.

"Sweet Jesus in Heaven. No. Ashley told me she didn't know who it was, and I wouldn't exactly call it a confrontation."

"What would *you* call it?"

"A tete-a-tete."

A tete-a-tete?" Ramsey.

"If my high school French serves me, a private conversation." Townsend.

"That's accurate," Pennington said.

"What was it about?"

"It was stupid, really. Pardon my language."

"How so?"

"He asked Ashley to dance and I took issue with it."

"You took issue with it?"

"Yes, I'm ashamed of myself. I shouldn't let my emotions get the better of me. I was brought up better than that. My sainted mother wouldn't be happy with me." And he wiped away a tear.

"And you didn't see anything?" Townsend.

"No, I didn't."

"Okay. I think we have enough. Thank you for your cooperation." Ramsey.

"Yeah. Thanks." Townsend.

"I want to make sure I do all I can. I couldn't live with myself if I knew something that could keep a violent killer from getting away with it and I didn't tell you. Are you sure that's all?"

"Yeah. I think so." Ramsey said. "We just needed you to clear up a couple of things for us and you've done that."

"Then I'll see you gentlemen out," Pennington said, rising. He wanted to get them out as quickly as possible.

At the door Townsend thanked him for his hospitality.

"Think nothing of it. I only wish I could have been more help."

"You helped us plenty," Ramsey said.

"Well, I'm happy for that."

On the elevator, this time the music was *Stairway to Heaven*, Ramsey said, "So what do you think?"

"He didn't do it."

"No?'

"That wimpy little bastard? My twelve-year-old daughter could kick his ass and she isn't even the toughest girl in her class."

***

Pennington called Ashley. "Did you tell those sons of bitches about me?"

"What?"

"Those god damn cops."

"Oh. No, I guess the Sage manager told them about your argument with him. I didn't even know who it was until they came to my office this morning. The news hasn't given out his name yet."

"Well, I know what his name was—asshole."

"Pennington, the poor man is dead."

"Yeah. I'm sorry." Without meaning it.

***

Pennington woke up oddly excited about seeing this Dr. Wu. After overnight reflection he was sorry for killing the guy and was hopeful that the acupuncturist could do something to help him with his aggression.

He drove through a Burger King and got a steak biscuit and black coffee on the way. After all those years of being a vegetarian he was really getting into the taste and texture of beef. And he decided real men should drink their coffee black.

The rush hour traffic leaving the perimeter was just as bad as that entering. But he reached Dr. Wu's office in good time. Immediately on entering, he heard soothing oriental music meant to calm patients nervous about treatments, playing on a small stereo system. He hoped it would work for him. As both a child and a young man he'd had a fear of needles and now he was on the verge of letting someone stick as many needles as she deemed necessary, into him. Obviously Dr. Wu's home as well as her clinic, he detected the smell of what he thought were Lima beans cooking, coming from the rear of the small house. He was surprised to be greeted by a blonde, middle aged caucasian male on entering.

"Good morning. I'm Christopher Spivey."

"Nice to meet you. Pennington, Penny, Wentworth."

"Welcome, Penny. We're happy to have you. I think you'll be pleased with your treatment. Dr. Wu is a miracle worker. In fact in addition to working for her I'm a patient of hers. She needed an office manager, someone to handle payables and receivables, take care of patients, answer the phones. I had a background in business management and was recently laid off and we came to an agreement."

The clinic had an array of artwork on the walls, ranging from depictions of Jesus, to oriental wall hangings, to charts indicating acupuncture needle placements in the body. The office area had shelves lined with jars painted with Chinese characters and filled with Asian pills and herbs used for additional treatments. Dr. Wu's sign fronting the building read Acupuncturist and Herbalist. Christopher picked up some forms from a desk and showed Pennington to exam room one. Two small former bedrooms in the small cottage had been partitioned off with curtains to form four smaller examination rooms. The hospital-style bed was sitting on cinder blocks and had a two-foot wide sheet of white paper running vertically down the middle. Pennington sat down, crinkling the clean, white paper, to complete the paperwork while he waited. As he wrote he heard someone, a woman, moaning in the next room. If the treatments caused her to moan in pain like that he wasn't sure about it.

Dr. Wu entered a few minutes later, her white lab coat swallowing her tiny form. Her eyes sparkled along with her happy smile. Her office manager handed her the forms Pennington had completed. After seeing their interaction, and even though he was probably close to twenty years younger than Dr. Wu, Pennington got the impression that theirs was more than just a professional relationship.

She extended a tiny, cadaver-like hand. "I'm Dr. Wu."

I'm Pennington Wentworth. I'm happy to meet you." He figured he should try to be nice to someone who was going to be sticking a bunch of needles in him, even though he now found being nice to be mentally taxing.

She looked over the paperwork and said, "You broke your head."

Pennington explained to her that he had a fractured skull and that he was experiencing severe personality change and aggression.

"I can work on that. I fix that before."

"You can fix it?"

"Probably take 6 months to one year. Come every week. But won't work unless you believe it work."

"Unless I believe it will work." He repeated as he inclined his head and pondered that. He thought he could decide later then, if he wanted it to work or not.

After getting acquainted she said they could start. She asked Pennington to remove his shirt and to lie down on his side on the hard bed, in much the same position as when getting a colonoscopy.

Dr. Wu started by taking a cotton ball pinched in a forceps and wiping down the areas with alcohol, in which she would insert the needles. She removed sharp tools from their small waxed paper packages and began to insert them into the skin on the top of his head. He couldn't be sure but he thought she used five or six. Then, moving to the top of his spine she inserted six needles. Pennington could tell the number of them due to the pain when she pressed them in a half to three quarters of an inch deep. "Oh, that hurts," he said. "Can you do it again?" he asked, enjoying it. Next, needles were inserted in the area of the liver. He thought the pain was exquisite and excruciating at the same time.

After finishing the process she said she'd be back and she gently left. Pennington tried to reach his iPad on the side table to entertain himself while she was out but when he attempted to move it was too painful for him, so he gave up on that idea. Since Christopher had led him to the examining room on the front of the house, the white noise from the traffic on the four lane highway the house fronted soon lulled him to sleep, only to be disturbed a few minutes later by the sound of a siren atop a passing ambulance.

After thirty minutes she returned and started to press with her hand to apply pressure on each of the needles. When Pennington flinched she said it wouldn't work unless it hurt. She said she was increasing his chi flow, even though he didn't know what that meant. "That's okay. I can handle it," he said.

After applying pressure to each one she said she'd be back and again left. Fifteen minutes later she returned and repeated the process of applying pressure to each needle. When he whimpered in pain after a particularly intense sensation, she said, "That's a good one." When another fifteen minutes had passed she returned to begin removing the needles with one hand, while at the same time wiping up the flowing blood with a cotton ball in the other.

Upon her finish, Pennington asked Dr. Lu, "By the by, how does acupuncture work?" She gave him the stock answer she gave non-Asians or anyone with no experience in the martial arts—that it would increase the flow of blood to the affected area. The true answer for Asians or those with a great deal of experience in the oriental fighting arts was that it would increase their chi flow, what orientals have long believed is the body's internal energy, its life force.

"And another question if I may—How long has acupuncture been around?"

"Not sure exactly, maybe 5,000-7,000 years."

"If that's the case, how was it done before the invention of needles?"

"At first, only pinch with fingers. That worked, but then use stick, then rock. Then sharpen stick and rock. That work better. Use that way for long time."

"Thank you, Dr. Wu. I was just curious."

As Pennington left, he heard the bark of a small dog coming from the rear of the house and through an open door, saw Dr. Wu sitting at a formica-topped kitchen table having a small bowl of rice for her lunch.

Since she'd told him he should eat something soon after the treatment Pennington decided to visit a nearby Korean restaurant for an early lunch. He chose galbi, a barbecue beef spare ribs dish with onions and scallions, and the small bowls of kimchi, sprouts, spicy green beans, fish balls and spicy cubed turnips that accompanied each dish.

Arriving home, and feeling weak after his treatment, he decided to relax with a glass of sweet Riesling on his small terrace and enjoy the view of the mountains.

Chapter 6
Getting Stronger

Pennington felt renewed physically when he awoke the morning after his first acupuncture regimen, but it took him most of the day to fully recover. She'd told him it would take at least twenty-four hours for him to rebound from the treatment. But then he felt better than he could ever remember. And he decided he should do something about his scrawny body. Even though he'd never paid any attention to it, he'd been passing a gym on Peachtree Industrial Boulevard for years. He knew nothing about weightlifting gyms but it looked like it might fill the bill. He didn't want a chrome and glass fern bar-type health club. He thought an old-school, concrete floor, un-airconditioned, unheated warehouse with rusty iron weights would be what he needed. He didn't want the type of club atmosphere where he'd have to associate with people like his former self. Try as he might, he couldn't escape the feeling that his brain change and accompanying personality changes were permanent.

Before he stepped foot in the gym he decided to go online and research workouts. He felt like he was too smart to ask anyone for help. That had been a problem for Pennington for awhile. Even though his wealth was inherited he looked down on people that were beneath him financially and felt that because he was wealthy that that somehow made him more accomplished and cleverer than others. And besides, he certainly wouldn't want to stoop to asking any of the meathead idiots of the type that would work at a gym for help. So, he was also guilty of stereotyping others as well, just like people did him.

Spending a couple of hours on the internet that morning helped him decide what he was going to do. Almost a foreign language with words like sets, reps, traps, lats and pecs, but with pictures and videos to help he decided that old school barbells and dumbbells and beginning with basic lifts that had been around and had been the staple of bodybuilders for more than a hundred years would probably be a better way to go than the myriad different, latest and greatest workouts designed by this expert or that PhD.

After a lunch of grilled steak to get some protein he drove to the no-name gym with a gravel parking lot and paint covered windows.

The first thing he noticed on entering was the the age of the building and the smell of sweat, rusty steel, and damp concrete. The guy who greeted him was definitely a meathead. Five foot nine inches tall and probably 250 pounds of orangutan-like muscle. Introduced himself as Bruno. Bruno's head was shaved and his neck was bigger than Pennington's leg and his shoulders looked like basketballs.

"I'm Penny," Pennington said, "Like in "bad" Penny." Even though with his beanpole thin body there was nothing bad or tough looking about him. "I'd like to join up."

"Why don't I show you around?" Bruno was proud of his gym and wanted Pennington to be impressed.

"I've seen enough."

With a skeptical look creasing his face, Bruno said, "You know we don't have machines here." Referring to ellipticals, stairmasters, treadmills or even fancy weight machines.

"That's fine. This is what I want."

Bruno explained the pricing options and said, "When do you want to start?"

"How about now?

"Okay, did you bring workout clothes?"

"Yep. I'll get 'em out of my ride."

Penny returned, gave Bruno cash for the first month, and the big guy directed him to the locker room in the rear. After changing into a yuppie-looking matching tank top and shorts ensemble, with a matching headband, and looking ridiculous—he still didn't have the whole tough guy image completely figured out—he came out and Bruno asked, "You need help with a program?"

"I think I can handle it," Penny said arrogantly and walked toward a flat bench with a forty-five pound seven foot olympic bar on the uprights. Already loaded with two forty-five pound plates for a total of one-hundred thirty-five pounds, the minimum that most men would start with. "Bad" Penny had to replace the forty-fives with twenty-fives for a very light, ninety-five pound starting weight. After getting five reps total, he was spent and racked the weight. Not a very auspicious beginning, but a beginning, nonetheless.

He moved to a corner with bars on the floor and using the olympic bar only, proceeded to do forty-five pound dead lifts, probably an all time record for feebleness.

The same kind of efforts and results were achieved on the standing shoulder press, the bent over row, squats and standing barbell curls.

After an hour and fifteen minutes he'd had enough. He hoped he had not passed the point where he'd regret it tomorrow, but already feeling the pain caused by the build up of lactic acid that he'd read about, he was afraid it was too late for that.

Got in his car and turned the borrowed Fiat in the direction of his condominium. Before getting far, though, a sign that read "tattoos" caught his eye. That would be a great addition to his transformation. Deciding there was no time like the present, he pulled up in front and went inside. Entering he thought, *yep, this is it.* A Latino with both arms, neck, and as much as you could see of his chest above his wife beater were covered in tats.

"Hector," he said.

"Bad Penny. I want a tattoo."

"Yeah, that's good. You need one. Make you look tough. Might take more than one for that, though," He had a sense of humor. "That's ok though. They become, how you say—addicting. Whatchu want, meng?"

"I was thinking a dragon, holding a penny in its mouth, maybe starting on my shoulder and going down my arm. How much?"

"For you meng, a special. $400.00."

"Let's do it."

There had been a lot of blood but it wasn't nearly as painful as the acupuncture had been. Hector bandaged the artwork and gave him a tube of Tattoo Goo to rub on the sensitive area three times a day for a week to keep it moist and help it heal. He got home and after his workout, and getting the tattoo and with his head still hurting, "Bad" Penny couldn't even make it to his bed. Dinner was a bloody red rare steak and then while sipping three fingers of Jack Daniels on the rocks, he collapsed on the sofa and watched mixed martial arts on his seventy inch Sony Vaio HD television, previously used for watching only chick flicks and comedies.

He slept fitfully, dreaming of his former self, effete, effeminate, vegetarian, pacifist, his Versace, and Gucci clothes, Prada shoes and Armani suits. He dreamt of the trip he took to New York City, to meet a girl in-person he'd met online. Took her to dinner at Milo's, a Greek seafood restaurant on W. 55th St. After the cost of airfare and a hotel, dinner for two with wine cost over four hundred dollars and he didn't even get a good night kiss out of the deal. In his dream he could smell the seafood from the restaurant mixed with the fragrance of his date's Tom Ford perfume.

He woke up pissed off, remembering the night.

***

Almost unable to move from the previous day's workout, after breakfast Penny decided to go back to Doraville for a massage at a Chinese massage studio he'd spotted. The sign out front advertised a grand-opening special. A half-and-half, described as a one hour, foot massage and full body combo for just forty dollars. So Penny decided to take advantage of the offering. Past the well-lit lobby, the rooms were dark, and quiet, with any speaking done at a whisper. The studio was decorated in traditional Chinese colors of red and gold in wall hangings and paintings. Quiet oriental music enhanced the authentic Chinese atmosphere. He sat down in a leather chair resembling a La-z-boy. A cute young Asian woman of about twenty-one brought a wooden pail lined with plastic and filled with hot water in which to soak his feet. After the soak, the chair was reclined and she started with his now clean, relaxed feet.

Like in acupuncture, pressure points on the feet corresponded to various parts and organs of the body, so the intense, hard pressure kneading, squeezing and stroking of the feet promoted health and wellness throughout the body.

Finishing with his feet and calves she moved around behind the chair to get to his face, head and shoulders. He discovered that the face massage was his favorite part. The pressing on his face around his mouth and gums, then moving to the area around his eye sockets, left him feeling invigorated and more energized than he could remember in a long time. Since he was still recovering from his fractured skull he told her not to work on his head. While still standing behind him she worked on his neck, shoulders and upper back.

Moving again to the front she lifted his arms, and shook them for a few moments before massaging his hands. Finishing with his upper legs, when Penny stood up to leave he was wobbly, but felt great.

***

Although he was sore the day after his first workout, Penny felt better the second day, especially after the massage on the off-day. So he was ready to work out again. As soon as he woke up he did a dozen pushups to get the blood moving in his body. Everything he'd read on the internet told him that he should try to increase the weight, number of reps, or number of sets in every workout. So armed with that information he returned to the gym ready to get stronger and bigger.

Entering the gym, Bruno greeted him warmly, but Penny felt sure that he looked at him with disdain. *I'll show him, the asshole, look down on me, will he.* He returned to the bench press, increased the weight by five pounds to one hundred and got two more reps for a total of seven. Surprised to see that, he was proud of himself and gave the air a fist pump, "Yes!" He got similar results in all of the exercises except the squats. He got only one more rep at the same weight.

Feeling good about his workout and confident, although his head still hurt, he decided to reward himself that night by going out to one of his favorite dance clubs. Dressed to the nines in an Armani suit, Prada dress shoes, appropriate accessories including a Gucci wallet and de Bleu by Chanel cologne, he went to the Andrews Entertainment Complex, found a parking spot and watched the people who entered ahead of him. The women beautiful and stuck up, the kind that never paid attention to him, the men that looked down on him because he wasn't masculine, although he could buy and sell them a hundred times over. As he watched, his anger and rage continued to build. Making the decision not to enter the club, he chose instead to feed his rage, to use it, to evolve into something that would terrify all those that looked down on him, or worse…ignored him.

Chapter 7
New Identity, New Digs

Bad Penny awoke for the last time in his penthouse condo and began poring over the AJC newspaper for a new car. Well, not *new*—or a car, per se —a used pickup not less than thirty years old would better suit his needs. Not finding what he was looking for, he got dressed and hit a trail of used car lots. At the third lot he visited, he hit paydirt. A 1982 Dodge Ram pickup. Painted brown, you couldn't tell where the paint ended and the rust began. Perfect. The engine started on the first attempt, meaning it ran better than it looked. Next to find a shitty apartment. His bat cave. Like Batman he had to be able to disappear, to blend in after his deeds, or in this case, his misdeeds. Nobody would confuse what he was planning with the Batman's heroic acts.

On a two lane street that ran west behind the Georgia Dome, home to the NFL's Atlanta Falcons, he found it—a one story cinder block building with six units. The hand-painted sign out front read "apartments" "by the day, week or munth". He would need to get a furnished unit.

An elderly African-American woman wearing a tattered purple, flower-print, cotton dress, sitting outside the first of the six doors stood up when she heard his muffler-less truck pull into the lot. She approached the truck and the smell of unfiltered cigarettes reached him before she did. Her cataract clouded eyes kept her from seeing him. That would work in his favor.

"Hep yuh?," she said.

"I need a place."

"I got one," she said. She was kind of a smart ass. He dug that about her. Her name was Myriam. "How long?'

"How much?"

"Hundred a week?"

"Furnished?"

"Course."

"How about a month in advance?"

"Three-seventy-five."

"Sold." He figured a month would give him time to do what he needed to do or he would be forced into retirement by law enforcement by then.

"He peeled off four Ben Franklins and said, "Keep the change.'

She held the bills an inch from her cataract-covered eye. He'd worried about cataracts in the past due to his sainted mother developing them at forty years old. Myriam gave him a gap-toothed grin.

The Goodwill Store he'd passed less than a mile away would provide him with his new wardrobe, faded blue denim dungarees, khaki-colored work shirts, tees, white socks, boots and a used plastic Timex to substitute for his Patek Philippe Celestial, the elegant six-figure timepiece that he'd bought as a present for himself after a particularly good week in the market. He had to try on boots until he found a pair that fit since he didn't know what size he wore.

Returning to his new digs, he couldn't remember exactly how he'd reached this place. Not the apartment—but this place in life. Afraid to even sit on the filthy chair covered in an orange- and yellow-striped corduroy fabric, he dressed while standing. As he was putting on the used jeans, used work shirt and lace up boots he was having flashbacks, pictures, snippets actually, of himself dressed in fine clothes and he was seeing a view of mountains but the vista was from far away because at that moment he couldn't remember a visit to mountains.

Early afternoon neared and he needed lunch. Pulling the filthy black-out curtain back he peered outside, and across the street and a couple of blocks away, he saw a diner-type, greasy food meat-and-three. It wouldn't take him five minutes to walk it. Get him out of the shitty apartment and into the fresh air.

The meatloaf didn't look as greasy as the fried chicken. So with sides of mashed potatoes and green beans flavored with bacon, cornbread and a huge glass of sweet tea, Bad Penny was full. His previously perfect table manners were non-existent. With a napkin stuffed in his shirt collar and both elbows on the table, a fork in one hand and a knife in the other, he shoveled food in as fast as his hands and mouth would let him. He wasn't accustomed to not having wine with a good meal but it wasn't a good meal. It nourished him and provided protein for building muscle and carbs for energy to do what he needed to do was all. While walking back to the apartment Bad Penny's cellphone trilled. Without even looking at the caller id, he chunked the expensive smartphone in a creek under the bridge he crossed without connecting the call. Couldn't have old "friends" calling him at an inconvenient time. Besides, they were never his friends. Not really. He was planning on upgrading his class of friends anyway. People more like Bad Penny himself. He would start working on that tonight.

This area of Atlanta boasted biker bars, strip clubs, cheap restaurants and cycle shops. He wondered what it'd be like to ride a Harley. He figured it'd be a new experience for him. Tonight he'd find some other experiences suiting his new life style.

The apartment had cold and colder running water, making his decision easy, so he decided on a cold shower, quickly exiting it and dry-shaved around the outline of his sparse beard using the cheap throwaway razor he'd picked up at a convenience store. He just shook his head to arrange his hair. It was getting longer. As soon as the sun went down he went out. He couldn't stand to spend too much time in that shitty apartment anyway. He decided a strip club would be his first stop. Since he didn't think he'd ever had sex with a woman, at least he could enjoy the show. He couldn't remember having been to a strip club before either. The neon sign on the cinder block building's front window read "Strip Club" and "Exotic Dancers." It was the type of joint one found in the seedier parts of town, not the higher end Buckhead gentlemens' clubs in which businessmen might entertain clients. He entered and took a seat at the foot of a small stage on the right side of the showroom. The announcer introduced "Cinnamon" dancing on the stage in front of him. He had a voice reminiscent of a 70's era FM disk jockey. Cinnamon was tall, probably over five-foot-nine and slender with long legs and the biggest pair of manmade breasts Penny'd ever seen. He guessed she took that sobriquet due to the color of the hair on her head since she didn't have hair anywhere else. Undulating before him, she said, "I'm Cinnamon."

"I heard. I'm Bad Penny."

"Oh, are you bad? I like bad boys."

"The baddest you've ever known, baby."

"Oooh."

He stuck a five in her garter as she squatted in front of him with her legs spread. He could only think of one other place he might insert it and he figured she probably wouldn't appreciate that. He was glad he'd had the foresight to get plenty of cash. Wouldn't be smart to use his American Express Black card. Wouldn't want to make it too easy for anyone to track him. He had several thousand dollars left even after paying cash for the beat up truck and a month in advance for the shitty apartment.

He made the mistake of peeling the five off a roll of bills that would choke a horse. Cinnamon wouldn't miss something like that and she wouldn't let him get away, now.

After dancing for Bad Penny for three songs in a row, she said, "I get off at 2—what are you doing later?

Penny said, "I've got some business to take care of, but I'll be done before 2.

"Lovely. Meet me back here and be ready to party."

"Sounds good baby." He figured that this was his chance to finally get some action with a real woman. "I'll be back."

Bad Penny drove to midtown, parked where he could observe the entrance of Lava, arguably Atlanta's most sophisticated lounge and dance club. And formerly one of his favorite nightspots. He recognized many of the faces entering, both male and female. And as he sat there he got more pissed off. He would definitely have to pay another visit, soon.

Chapter 8
The Attacks

Bad Penny thought he might as well return to the strip club and enjoy the show until Cinnamon's night was done. Who knows—he might find someone he liked better.

All the dancers had breast implants. Apparently it was a job requirement. The financial enthusiast he'd been in his previous life wondered if they were a tax deductible job expense.

He thought Cinnamon was the most attractive and a good choice for what he thought would be his first sexual experience. He had a couple of beers to curb his enthusiasm, so to speak.

It wasn't long before Cinnamon approached him from the rear of the club. She had put on clothes—wore skin tight jeans, six-inch high heeled tres chic Jimmy Choo stilettos and a zebra skin tank top. He liked this look almost as well as seeing her nude.

"Follow me?"

"Aiiight," Bad Penny said.

He followed her to a small car, a Mini Cooper S, and she drove him to his truck. He was a little embarrassed by the rust-bucket pickup, but *she's a God damn stripper. Who gives a fuck what she thinks?*

He followed her to a quiet in-town neighborhood near Georgia Tech where she parked on the street in front of a surprisingly traditional fifties-era bungalow encircled by the proverbial white picket fence. He wasn't sure what kind of home he expected a stripper to have but he chastised himself for having made assumptions about her.

"Come on in," she said in a singsongy voice from the sidewalk. Once inside she closed the front door, leaned against it and licked her lips. "How about a glass of chard?'

Penny said, "how about a bourbon, on the rocks, three fingers?"

"You sure? You look like a chardonnay drinker to me."

"Used to be. Gave it up for lent," he said, His wit was still on point.

"Funny. You don't look Jewish."

He was embarrassed by her stupidity but figured this wouldn't be a long-term relationship. And he knew her mouth would be too busy to do much talking anyway.

Cinnamon poured him a glass of bourbon, said, "You know this date is going to cost you."

"How much?

"Five hundred?"

"Aiiight." Remembering the NYC date when he spent four big ones for dinner, plus airfare and hotel and didn't even get a kiss—he figured this was a pretty good deal—and pulled out five Ben Franklins. Besides, he also knew he'd be getting it back later.

Cinnamon put the cash in her purse and took Penny by the hand and led him to the bedroom. "Let's take a shower first." She undressed him, then herself and they entered the recently remodeled bathroom. The door to a standalone, glass shower that had room for two was open. The textured, pebble inlaid floor of the shower would provide good footing for shower action he anticipated.

Penny kissed her and she took him in her hands and lathered him up. After a couple of minutes of this she "accidentally" dropped the soap. Squatting down to retrieve it, she took him into her mouth. He caressed her face with both hands and began thrusting into her face. Being his first time, it was less than thirty seconds before he exploded into her mouth. She licked her lips and swallowed. After he recovered in seconds though, she said "wow" and led him to the bed. "I've never seen anyone orgasm and keep their erection like that." She was impressed. He smiled, pleased with himself.

"Thanks. It was nothing."

They moved to the bed and Cinnamon pushed him down on his back and straddled him, sliding him deep inside her wetness. "Come on baby. Give it to me. Give it to me,"she said.

Reaching up, Bad Penny took her face in his hands, touching it gently, then moving them slowly down to her creamy white neck, his hands encircled her throat—tighter, tighter, until she realized what was happening.

"I'll give it to you, you fucking bitch. Think you can make me pay for it. I can have any god damn woman I want."

Sheer terror in her eyes. An expression of anguish from her red-painted mouth.

As he choked the life out of her, he said, "Don't take it personally baby. This is just practice. You weren't anything special. It could have been anybody."

Once it was over he felt more exhilaration by Cinnamon taking her last breath in his hands than he did by his first sexual experience.

He was left to the task of cleaning up. First, he dressed, and then, retrieving a towel from the bathroom, he wet it under the faucet and wiped down every surface with which he'd come in contact and took the glass that held the bourbon, with him. He was not overly concerned about fingerprints though, because he knew he'd never been fingerprinted and so knew there'd be no record of him in IAFIS, the national fingerprint system maintained by the FBI.

And he wasn't at all worried about any prints on her throat because from all of the reading he'd done for pleasure he knew that contrary to what you see in television and movies, getting usable prints off of skin was challenging at best and damn near impossible to do at worst.

While cleaning and seeing no additional clothes in the spare bedroom or no sign of anyone else, Penny decided she didn't have a roommate, so more than likely no one would miss her until she didn't show up for work the next night.

***

Bad Penny slept in, exhausted from his late night of terror. When he did wake up he felt exhilarated, more alive than he could ever remember. He thought that was ironic, killing someone making him feel so alive. After strong coffee, black, he decided to go to the gym, get a workout. As he drove, all he could think about was that he needed to build up his strength. Although it wasn't that hard to choke the shit out of a chick—he was acting on pure adrenaline—depending on the sex of his next victim and how he decided to do it, it was possible he would need more power.

He wore a cheap blue and red Atlanta Braves cap he'd picked up at a service station with the bill pulled low over his eyes. A rolled towel around his neck and iPod earbuds in his ears. Wanted people to leave him alone so he could focus. He wanted to increase the weight and reps on each exercise. Success! One-hundred and five pounds for 8 reps on bench. And increases on standing military press, barbell curls, squats, dead lift and bent over rows. He was beginning to feel like a real bad ass.

He would use the next two nights scouting out nightspots to be ready to strike on the weekend.

***

Dressed in jeans, a black wife beater tank top and work boots, riding in his crappy pickup, Bad Penny was practically invisible. Parking in a dark corner of a lot at one of the many popular in-town clubs in Atlanta, he pulled out the thermos of coffee he'd filled at a service station. It sucked. He missed Starbuck's lattes. After drinking half the thermos of coffee he got out of the crappy truck to piss. At the rear edge of the lot under the cover of darkness, he pissed against a tree trunk, intuitively knowing that peeing vertically against the trunk would be quieter than pissing on the flat ground.

Getting back in the crappy truck and after inserting his iPod earbuds he listened to *Helter Skelter,* the music of the Charles Manson murders and he'd even found some recordings by the man himself, Manson, who'd been a little known musician before he became one of the world's most famous cult leaders. Bad Penny felt that Manson had a smooth voice and played a decent acoustic guitar, but was disappointed in how light and airy some of his music was. He'd assumed it would be darker. With his new fuller beard and longer hair, Penny even thought that he himself bore a passing resemblance to Manson.

After listening to *Helter Skelter* four times…He perked up.

"God damn!"

Even though he was twenty-five years older, Bad Penny recognized one of his chief tormentors from grade school, Mark Spalding. He'd been much like Pennington himself, effeminate even at ten years old, but he'd used that as fuel to persecute those he felt were even weaker than he. And Pennington was the only one weaker than him. The two of them were usually the last ones chosen for sports teams at recess, even after the girls. Pennington never got over that and he felt like it contributed to him being unsuccessful in business, life and relationships.

Tears came to Penny's eyes and flooded down his cheeks as he thought about his unhappy childhood and his dearth of friends. His best friend was a neighbor's dog, Champ, and he hung out with the animal more than any of the kids in the neighborhood.

Now he knew his next victim.

He was bored waiting for Mark, sure the son of a bitch was drinking, partying and chatting up chicks. He hoped he would leave the club alone. *Although what would be the harm in one more murder?*

Just before the spookiest hour of the night Bad Penny saw him again. Leaving alone. The night was getting ready to turn spooky for Spalding. Everything in his life was getting ready to fall apart.

Spalding was walking in his general direction, toward a two or three-year-old, silver Mazda sedan. *Typical, no imagination at all.*

Bad Penny exited his truck and walked toward him at a ninety-degree angle.

"Spalding," he said in an outdoor voice.

"Do I know you?"

You ruined my life and you don't know me? "Pennington Wentworth."

A moment searching the recesses of his memory, then, "Pennington. Good to see you."

Yeah, you think it's good to see me. "You, too."

"So, what're you doing?"

"Waiting for a friend."

"Well, it's good to see you. I gotta jet." Spalding obviously didn't care to get involved in a long conversation.

"You, too. Take care."

Spalding turned his back on Penny and focused his attention to opening his car door.

Bad Penny moved silently and swiftly, pulling a butcher knife from his belt as he moved. He snaked his arm around Spalding and pressed the stiletto-sharp knife against his throat. Penny could immediately smell the stench of shit as Spalding's bowels released.

"Man, what'd you do that for? That fucking stinks."

"I couldn't help it. I'm scared. What are you doing this for?" His voice quavering.

"I've never gotten over how you treated me."

"We were kids, man. It was just stupid, harmless kid stuff."

"Harmless? Look at me. I'm thirty-five years old and I'd never been with a woman til last night. I don't have a career. If my father hadn't had money I don't know how I'd live. My life has sucked and it started with you."

"But…but think about it. If you hurt me, you're life will be over."

"Just shut up and get in the god damn truck. It doesn't look like much but at least it doesn't stink." But it would with this fucker's pants full of shit.

Spalding started sobbing. "No, no, don't make me."

"Get in the god damn truck," he repeated. "I won't say it again."

This time he complied, although due to his being paralyzed by horror, he could barely pull himself up in the passenger side seat.

Going around and climbing behind the wheel, Bad Penny had to find somewhere remote, somewhere isolated, so he could do what he needed to do.

Thinking back to when he was a teenager, he remembered that the cool kids used to go to the old Oakland Cemetery near downtown Atlanta late at night to hangout and try to scare each other the way kids will do. It would be a perfect place. Surely no one else would be there after midnight on a week night, so he could commit his act of terror and move on.

Oakland was the final resting place for many noted Atlantans including championship golfer Bobby Jones, literary great and author of *Gone with the Wind,* Margaret Mitchell, and many former Atlanta mayors and politicians. Due to the many civil war dead buried there as well, stories of ghosts were common.

Bad Penny pulled up to the front gate on Memorial Drive. Shining the crappy truck's one headlight on the gate, he could see the large lock holding the twin iron gates shut. Got out and searched the rear of the truck until he found a tire iron. Covered with rust, it was original to the truck. With his newfound strength it didn't take him long to breach the lock, and the chain dropped to the ground with a loud rattle. Dogs barked at the noise unnerving the still. He hoped it wouldn't wake the unconscious neighbors of Oakland. He turned off the light of the truck to reduce the visibility. Entered through the gate and drove past the dark visitor center and on the circular asphalt paved drive, drove to the rear of the large cemetery and forced Spalding out of the truck at knife point. An ethereal crescent moon was partially exposed behind the columnar-shaped Westin Peachtree Plaza, the second tallest hotel in the Western Hemisphere.

Finding a tomb that was large enough for his purpose, at the point of the knife, Bad Penny forced Spalding to lie down on the concrete slab. Shadows from the moonlight hitting the skeletal trees cast over them and the tombstone.

"Pennington, don't," Spalding shrieked.

"Who's this Pennington? I'm Bad Penny."

Thinking he had an opening, because Pennington seemed confused, he said, "Pennington, it's me, your old school friend, Mark, Mark Spalding."

"I don't know you. I just know you're an effeminate bastard and you piss me off and you're going to die." Bad Penny knelt beside his victim and held the sharp butcher knife to Spalding's throat. "Die bitch." And he tore and slashed the knife across his throat. He heard the guy's trachea rip and before he died, the gushing wound rasped as it tried to take in life-giving oxygen to no avail. A three foot pool of blood quickly covered the concrete slab. As Bad Penny raised up he buried the six inch blade to the hilt into the guy's heart.

Not knowing where he was or how he got there, Bad Penny rose from where he knelt. All he knew was he enjoyed watching the blood erupt from this wimpy, girl-like person's throat. He felt a growing erection at the sight of the gore. The transformation from sweet, effeminate, pacifist, Pennington Wentworth, II, to Bad Penny, serial murderer, was complete. And he remembered nothing of his life from before the first murder.

Getting in the crappy truck after 1:00 a.m., he drove without direction until dawn. Returning to the shitty apartment only long enough to wash the blood from his body in the shower and change into workout clothes, he then left driving toward the no-name gym. Deciding to stop at a Waffle House, the Atlanta headquartered chain restaurant known for its breakfasts, as far as he knew having never been there before, he was surprised to see those coming off the midnight shift, strippers getting off work and white-collar professionals on their way to the office early, rubbing shoulders, like him, while there for breakfast. He ordered fried eggs, bacon, hash browns, pancakes and about a gallon of coffee, and ate like it was his last meal. He was unsurprisingly hungry after his late night. Back in the truck, radio on, the local news had reports of his past two night's escapades. The APD was investigating, but the news reader said there didn't appear to be a connection. That was good news for him.

Bruno met him with a nod and a "howyadoin." More of a greeting, not really wanting to know.

"Mornin." His own without enthusiasm, was no more than an acknowledgement that he saw someone.

A dude working out on the lat pull down machine inclined his head in Bad Penny's direction, earning him an icy glare in return.

He was motivated beyond words for his workout. It could only be the adrenaline rush and the thrill he got from killing. He made big increases in weight and reps in all his exercises. And the good thing about being thin was he was already seeing ropey muscles pop out.

***

Saturday morning and he decided to go to reconciliation, more commonly known as confession. Even though he couldn't know for sure, he innately believed he was Catholic. So he should confess his sins, do his best to save his eternal soul from damnation. He looked up Catholic Churches on the internet and tried to find a large one so hopefully a parish priest wouldn't recognize him from the past if he'd been a parishioner, or remember him in the future if he returned.

From what he could find, Cathedral of Christ The King was the largest parish in Atlanta and one of the ten largest in the U.S. Hopefully no one would recognize him or remember him.

The church's website said reconciliations were heard from noon until 2:00 on Saturdays. He decided to show up just before two o'clock hoping there'd be fewer people around.

Fortunately Monsignor Francis O'Brien heard reconciliations in the confessional and not in his office. So the priest couldn't see him. That was good even though he knew that priests were sworn to secrecy within the confines of the confessional.

An elderly woman entered the booth ahead of him. He made sure to avoid her sight. It didn't take her long and Bad Penny entered.

He cracked the door and heard, "Enter, my child."

"Thank you, Father."

Bad Penny made the sign of the cross, and said, "In the name of the Father, and of the Son and of the Holy Spirit." He said, "Father, I don't remember how long its been since my last confession."

The holy man read a passage of holy scripture.

After the scripture reading Bad Penny continued, "I have killed three people." Then he confessed the fornication with the stripper, Cinnamon.

The Monsignor said, "Oh dear," which was not the norm in the progression of the Act of Reconciliation. As a penance he told Bad Penny to recite the Rosary. Then the holy man helped him through an

Act of Contrition. He then recited the words of absolution: *God, the Father of Mercies, through the death and resurrection of his son has reconciled the world to himself and sent the Holy Spirit among us for the forgiveness of sins; through the ministry of the church may God give you pardon and peace, and I absolve you from your sins, in the name of the Father, and of the Son, and of the Holy Spirit.* The confession ended:

The high priest: "Give thanks to The Lord, for he is good."

Bad Penny with Monsignor Francis's help, said: "His mercy endures forever."

He thanked the gentle man and, his eternal soul saved, he exited the confessional. Wondering if he could truly trust the holy man gave him pause. Looking around and seeing no one else in the sanctuary he crept to the altar and after selecting a heavy, solid gold chalice encrusted with jewels, made his way back to the confessional, ripped open the door to the priest's compartment and began to beat him unmercifully. And even though the he was dead by the third strike, Bad Penny continued to club him thirty additional times, until blood drenched the floor of the closet-sized compartment.

Every square inch of his clothes were soaked in blood. He had to find an exit out of the church other than the front door. Saturday vigil mass didn't start until five o'clock so luckily for Bad Penny the church and its grounds were mostly empty.

Making his way back to the altar area he found an exit out the rear of the church. He inched the door open, and peeking outside, the only person he saw was a groundskeeper riding a large mower. He waited until the lawn-man made a turn on the expanse to go back in the opposite direction, then Bad Penny made his break for the parking lot. Sprinting as hard as he could with his still injured legs, his heart was exploding in his chest.

Gaining the truck, he sat for a moment—breathing deep, calming himself, resisting the urge to scream out of the lot, engine racing and tires squealing, calling attention to himself. He forced himself to pull out slowly.

∗∗∗

Getting dressed to go out and seek more victims, Bad Penny was positively ecstatic. His latest attack satisfied him emotionally, physically and sexually. The prospect of a Saturday night on the town in Atlanta got him excited. He knew there would be large numbers of beautiful women clubbing—having fun drinking and dancing. A target rich environment. He didn't know why he hated these women but he knew he would be unable to rest until he satisfied his bloodlust.

He needed some new clothes, nothing fancy, but some pants, a shirt and tie and a sport coat so he could go into some of these places rather than just sitting in his truck, watching. Wanting to conserve his cash, he went to Suit City. It took him less than thirty minutes to pick out a suit, shirt, tie, socks and belt and he spent less than one hundred, twenty-five dollars. And might have found someone else who needed killing. The clerk, a god damn brown-skinned Indian, for God's sake, disrespected him.

He needed to find some cheap dress shoes. Remembered seeing some place called Shoe Land on his drive to the gym.

A hand-painted sign read "No Shoes over $25.00". His kind of place. He selected a no-name-brand pair of black leather lace-ups that would pass a cursory inspection in the dark and he was set. Spent $19.95 plus tax. His previous self wore nothing but Prada dress shoes that cost thousands but fortunately for him he couldn't remember those days. Less than a mile away he pulled into a gas station, the old-style kind with the restroom around back, got the key from the attendant and changed in the bathroom stall. He stuffed his old clothes in the trashcan since he knew he had four more outfits just like that one.

Opting for dinner at the strip club where he met Cinnamon, he could kill sometime before the nightclubs started hopping and for the price of a couple of beers, eat at its free buffet.

The buffet table was loaded down with meatballs in barbecue sauce, American cheese, crackers, chips and pretzels. Low quality, cheap and loaded with carbs—and filling. No one seemed to remember him from the night he killed Cinnamon, so he felt safe. After a couple of beers loosened him up he wanted a lap dance. A stunning blonde watched him move to a table near her stage and set her sights on him.

She approached him. "I'm Jezebel. What's your name?"

"Er…Jim, Jim Smith." Just in case Cinnamon told anyone she was leaving with Penny.

"Nice to meet you Jim. Want a dance?"

"Sure."

She said, "I don't remember seeing you here before."

"I'm new in town." The truth was he didn't know or remember anything from before about a week previously.

"Where are you from?"

"Tampa." It was the first place that popped into his mind.

"Ooh, I love the beach."

The next song, Rod Stewart's *Do You Think I'm Sexy* started and she began a lap dance. When she finished he gave her a ten and stood up.

"I've got to go darlin.' "

"Well, come back to see me, Jim."

"You know it baby."

He walked out. "Well shit."

A policeman providing security was walking the parking lot when Bad Penny left. The officer glanced his way. Nothing. No look of recognition or even curiosity. The police didn't know him.

***

He could stalk his prey tonight free from worry about whether he was on the radar screen of law enforcement.

From what Bad Penny could find on the internet Tongue & Groove was considered by many to be the best night club in Atlanta. There was no cover charge before eleven o'clock so he would save that twenty dollars.

Parking in the dark garage next door he thought that it could be opportunistic for what he anticipated were his late night plans. He put T&G's dress-to-impress slogan to the test with his cheap suit, cotton/poly-blend white shirt and his polyester tie, but in the dim light outside the door, the bouncer tending the velvet rope either had bad eyesight or felt sorry for him.

The first T&G opened in '94 and this one was a new and improved, larger version. Practically continuous in its operation since '94, made it The ATL's longest running dance club. Bad Penny sat down at the first of the three bars he came to.

The bartender took his order—a jack-and-coke.

When he returned with his drink Penny asked him, "What time does this joint get cranked up?

"Not before midnight."

"Well, shit." He didn't feel like wasting time in the club no matter how classy it was. Wanted to find a chick, satisfy his bloodlust and get the hell out of Dodge. This wasn't his kind of place. The guys were too straight-laced and the women looked stuck up.

Bad Penny finished his drink but opted for one more to see if the night picked up before he checked out.

Before his second drink arrived a hot thirty-year-old sat down at the bar, not in the seat next to him, but two stools down, didn't want him to think she was interested. She was dressed to kill. Bad Penny knew nothing about women's clothes, designers or anything of the sort—only a fag would know something like that, he thought, but he could tell the skirt, blouse, stiletto pumps and handbag were expensive. She had that air about her. Money, but probably daddy's money.

He casually looked over and gave her his best naughty-boy smile and said, "How you doin?"

Hello," she replied.

"I'm Penny."

"Sheryl. That's an unusual name."

"Nice to meet you, Sheryl. Family name—my great grandfather's—he was a civil war hero." Truth was he didn't even know if he had a family, or friends, for that matter. But he was glib and could think on his feet and was getting better at it.

"That's interesting." She thought if he had on a better suit, and got a shave, and a better haircut, he'd be handsome. Like a young Nicholas Cage. Still there was something about him, sexy, that bad-boy look.

"Can I buy you a drink?" He thought it would be a worthwhile investment if this played out the way he hoped.

"I'd love one. A cosmopolitan."

"You got it. Bartender, the lady wants a cosmo."

The bartender, dressed better than Penny, gave him a look like "listen to the loser in the cheap suit."

"So, what do you do Penny?"

"Personal protection."

"Personal protection? What's that?"

"You'd call me a bodyguard. So you're in good hands, baby."

"That's good. I don't want to take any chances."

They made small talk, had another drink and danced to a couple of tunes.

"Penny, I need to get up early. Would you mind seeing me to my car?" She didn't want to go into that creepy, dark parking garage alone.

"It'd be my pleasure." This was working out even easier than he'd hoped. *Chicks are so stupid; leave with a stranger she just met in a bar.* It was fortuitous that she parked in the same dark garage as Bad Penny. They took the elevator up to the second floor. He kissed her as the slow-moving lift made its ascent. They exited and as she led him toward her car, a small Porsche Boxter, he loosened his tie.

She unlocked the door using the key fob and at the driver's side turned and kissed Bad Penny.

"Call me?"

"What do you think?"

He moved in to kiss her again and as he did, in one deft move, grabbed one end of the polyester tie, pulled it from the loose collar and using both hands, quickly looped it around her neck. Her eyes registered the shock and confusion he knew she must be feeling as he pulled on both ends with all the strength of which he was capable. He kissed her on both of her bulging eyes and when she stopped struggling, and breathing, shoved her inert body into the chick car.

"God damn bitch shouldn't have been so stupid. She deserved to die," he muttered to himself, retying the tie as he walked toward his own crappy truck.

Chapter 9
A Different Approach

Bad Penny was growing tired of nightclubs. His suit gave him an idea. Approach professional women on their turf. First though, finding an old school barbershop was a challenge, because almost all you could find in Atlanta weere fancy-schmancy salons and spas. But his first order of business on Monday morning was to get a businessman's haircut.

The red-and-white striped barber pole outside the small shop was the sign he'd found what he was looking for. The old-fashioned bell that jingled when it was hit by the opening door confirmed it.

"Hep yuh?" the man in his eighties, standing by the one chair, asked.

"Haircut?"

"Hop up," he said, gesturing to the chair and popping the cape he would tie around Bad Penny's neck. A small black and white television made in the previous century sat in the corner and a news commentator from one of the local stations, who was trying to make it to CNN was talking about the sudden rash of killings in Atlanta. The police said at first there didn't appear to be a connection between them, but their investigation revealed what appeared to be a link.

Penny did as he was told and said, "How long ya been cutting hair?"

"Durn near sixty years."

"Long time."

"Durn long time. Cut the greatest president in the history of the union's hair, Dwight D. Eisenhower, back in '57 when he passed through town. Cut Andy Griffith's hair too when he used to be an Atlanta lawyer on that tv program. Cut Bobby Cox's hair and Joe Torre's when they was managers of the Braves."

God, I wish he'd shut up, Bad Penny thought. *I might have to make sure he doesn't talk too much in the future.*

"I've got five grandkids and twelve great grandkids. Want to see their pitchers?"

"That's aiiight." *Oh God, please make him stop,* he thought.

Finally he ended his inane pratter. "That'll be a sawbuck," he said.

Bad Penny gave him an Alexander Hamilton. And as the old man turned his back to put the bill in the old-style cash register, Penny pulled the knife that he now carried everywhere, and stabbed him in the spine, just above his skinny old white ass. Paralyzed him and killed him instantaneously. He wiped off the blood spray from his hand with the green and white-striped barber's cape that the old man'd tossed on the chair. Penny hadn't planned on killing him, but the octogenarian had annoyed the hell out of him with his incessant droning. He just couldn't help himself. He walked to the door and looked both directions and not noticing anyone in the small strip center parking lot, exited. As he walked out the door he called over his shoulder, "You shouldn't've talked so goddamn much."

                                    ***

Now Bad Penny could move to different fertile grounds to find his next victim. And change his pattern in case law enforcement was staking out nightclubs. He stopped into a dry cleaners and had his suit pressed while he waited and then dropped by Suit City and bought another white shirt. And another tie since the other one was pretty threadbare from using it to strangle Sheryl. The clerk was still a shit and he reminded himself he might have to return at closing time some night and teach him the error of his ways.

He went back to the shitty apartment, couldn't figure out why he lived there. Figured only a loser would live in a place like that, but he knew he wasn't a loser. He might not be real educated, he didn't know, or couldn't remember, but he could tell he was good at figuring things out.

Only early afternoon, he took a nap and dreamed. Saw himself wearing expensive clothes, in a fine apartment and with pretty girls. He couldn't put it altogether, but he knew he'd been different before and something'd caused him to lose his memory, and that he and this brain that was so aggressive, were new to each other.

Bad Penny decided that some of the higher end hotels in Atlanta should offer lots of options for targets. It was just a short, fifteen minute drive from the shitty apartment to downtown Atlanta, where the Marriott Marquis, the Hyatt Regency and the Atlanta Hilton, were within a five minute walk of each other. He was too embarrassed to give a valet the crappy pickup so he self-parked it in one of the lots on

Peachtree St. surrounded by a chain linked fence topped with razor wire.

He decided first to check out the lobby bar at the Hilton. When you entered the Hilton, upon walking into the lobby you made an immediate u-turn to the left to enter the bar. It was a large watering hole to accommodate the huge numbers of business people that stayed in the hotel, and on this Monday night the bar was fairly crowded with business men and women of all ages and colors who were winding down after a hard day at the office or of travel and sales calls and relaxing with an adult beverage. Penny selected a place where he could lean against the bar and ordered a bone-dry Tito's martini up. He wished he had a cell phone and a briefcase to act as props, but if this night were successful, he'd get those to use next time.

Scouting out the possibilities, he noticed two separate women who were alone. One down the bar from him and one sitting by herself at a table. His target had to be alone or whomever she were with could place him with the victim. He knew most others didn't pay attention to anything going on around them. Both attractive, the one at the bar was about forty, with dishwater blonde hair and wore a business suit, jacket and skirt, in navy blue that appeared to be custom tailored with a cream colored silk blouse. Like him, she was drinking a martini, up. The one sitting alone at a table was Asian, appeared to be either Korean or Vietnamese, mid-to-late thirties, petite and very cute, wearing a floral print dress in spring colors. She was drinking a glass of white wine, most likely chardonnay, based on the color. Bad Penny told the bartender to give the woman at the bar another martini of whatever type she was drinking, and he sent another glass of wine to the Asian woman and then waited to see who bit first.

After the bartender set a martini on the bar in front of her, bar woman acknowledged him with an incline of her head then turned the other direction. A clear brush-off.

He turned his attention toward the Asian chick. She gracefully accepted the glass of chardonnay, (he'd noticed the bottle of Cakebread when the bartender placed it in the tableside chiller) and gestured for Bad Penny to join her at her table.

Penny sauntered over with an air of insouciance, setting the pain in his legs aside and putting the coolest gait of which he was capable on show.

"Hi, I'm Elliott," he said.

"I'm Tess."

"Nice to meet you Tess."

'You too. Thanks for the drink. Join me?"

"You're very welcome. Don't mind if I do. What brings you here?" he asked as he pulled out the chair.

"I'm a government contractor, down from D.C., calling on the local military bases.

"Interesting," he said. *Just shoot me now.*

"What do you do?"

"Importer/Exporter. Small household goods, accessories, brick-a-brack from southeast Asia to this country and anything they want going back their way." He was making it up on the fly.

"We're in a similar industry then. I sell anything they could possibly need to the federal government. Are you staying here in the hotel?"

"No. I'm at the Hyatt. Had a meeting here though. A presentation for a group of clients." His story got more involved as he told it.

"I see."

They made small talk for the better part of an hour and then Penny suggested, "I've got an idea. There's a nice revolving, rooftop bar at the Hyatt. You want to try it?"

"I've heard about it. It sounds lovely, but I need to get out of these work clothes, get into something more comfortable. Give me a minute?"

"No problem."

"Be back shortly,"

She uncrossed her perfect legs, exited the bar and crossed the large lobby to the bank of high-speed elevators that would take her to the executive floors for Hilton's best customers.

Getting tired of waiting and wanting to act on his plan, Bad Penny was beginning to think she'd changed her mind, but after a half hour she returned. The flowery print dress was gone and she wore tight white jeans and a purple top that had see-through mesh on the shoulders and arms and very high matching purple heels with pointy toes—very hot.

"Miss me?" she asked.

"More than you know." He stood up and straightened the lapels of his cheap suit.

"Hmmmh, good," she said, nuzzling him. She'd reapplied her perfume and touched up her makeup while she was in the room.

The Hyatt was two blocks west and less than a five minute stroll. Along the way Bad Penny noticed the entrances to two dark alleys that could present interesting possibilities.

***

Although the oldest of the major hotels in downtown Atlanta, the Hyatt Regency had been continuously updated and had aged gracefully. As they walked through the lobby, even on a Monday evening, the grand old lady was a beehive of activity, with people enjoying southern cooking in the first floor restaurant, "Sway", drinking at the large lobby bar, standing in line at the Starbucks or milling around taking pictures and gazing skyward at the twenty floors of guest rooms that looked inward to the lobby. The menagerie of foreign languages they heard caused one to think this was not a hotel in the southern US, but one in any number of countries in Europe. Bad Penny heard an Eastern European language, a Canadian accent and recognized Italian speech, although he didn't know how he knew. A nearly forty-foot diameter round skylight, two hundred feet above, helped to illuminate the lobby floor with early evening moonlight.

Bad Penny and Tess took one of the six fast-rising, all glass elevators to the rooftop lounge that had recently been remodeled and reopened after being closed for almost a decade. The lobby quickly fell away as the lift made its heart-stopping ascent. Penny's stomach rose into his throat as he watched the floor get smaller.

The Polaris Lounge had been a popular place for locals and tourists alike after it's opening in the late sixties. It's exterior blue glass and flying saucer-like shape atop the Hyatt drew people from all over the south to view the architectural wonder. When constructed the Hyatt was the tallest building in several states and the view of the green Georgia countryside was breathtaking. Now surrounded on all sides by taller buildings, the view, while still worth the trip to the top, wasn't as spectacular.

Inside it had been restored and even surpassed its previous glory from six decades earlier. The Polaris made a full revolution every forty-five minutes so where one sat didn't matter as there would be a view of all directions in just a short time. Tess and Bad Penny got a table for two right next to the wall of windows and waited for the scenery to change. A few minutes after taking their order, the young, attractive blonde server returned with a house chard for Tess and an extra dry Grey Goose martini for Bad Penny.

Tess told Penny about her life, her large Vietnamese family in Baltimore, brothers and sisters—she was the eldest, her mother owned a nail salon. Her mom didn't do nails anymore herself, but still ran the shop. Bad Penny had to try to change the subject or bored to tears, he'd have to kill her, or himself, immediately. He asked her about movies she'd seen and at least that wasn't as bad. He couldn't remember any of the films she mentioned. But at least he thought he'd be able to wait until later to kill her instead of doing it right there in front of anyone.

Tess ordered another white wine and then left for the restroom. When the server returned with the drink order he asked her for a straight coke. He didn't want to get too drunk before he killed the pretty Asian. He wanted to remember the deed.

She returned to the table.

'I've been doing all the talking. Where are you from?"

He didn't want to talk about himself because he didn't know anything about his past and he'd have to make it up on the fly. "Dallas."

"Really? You don't look like a Texan."

"I shit you not.

"Do you have a family?"

"A married brother with four kids and four dogs. I love my nieces and nephews, two legged and four legged variety, dearly." He thought, *Damn I'm good at making this shit up.*

She said, "I have nieces and nephews also. They're so much fun. I just love spending time with them."

The conversation dragged until Bad Penny said, "I guess I should get you back to your hotel."

"Good idea—I have an early meeting in the morning." Tess was a go getter but didn't need a lot of sleep. She would get up early and go to the hotel gym first and put some time in on the treadmill and do yoga like most days, whether at home or out of town on business.

He paid the check and they took their leave. Tess thought it odd that he paid the bill with cash since most businesspeople used credit cards.

His heart pounded deeply in his chest and his breathing quickened as he anticipated his action. As he thought about the previous attacks and enjoying it more every time, he knew he'd never be able to stop.

It was a cool spring night so that would aid Bad Penny in his plans. She wasn't dressed for the cool late night and he noticed her shiver. Half a block up the sidewalk he said, "Let's cut through this alley. It'll be quicker. Get you out of this chilly weather."

"Do you think it's safe?"

"I'm sure it is. It'll come out directly beside your hotel." *You only have to concern yourself with me, baby.*

"Okay then." She still wasn't sure but she thought he seemed capable of taking care of them if need be.

About seventy-five feet down the alleyway it took a ninety degree turn to the left. Right at that corner was a dumpster. The deepest, darkest part of the alley. Bad Penny leapt on to her with cat-like quickness and lean strength. Covering her mouth with one hand and bouncing her head off the concrete he pounded her unmercifully with his other hand and elbow and kneed her in the stomach and ribcage. Cracking her skull, breaking her ribs, knocking out several teeth, breaking her nose and blackening both eyes, she was short moments from death. The beautiful Asian woman she'd been would be unrecognizable to anyone that knew her.

Finished and satisfied with his terror, he threw her, moments from death, into the dumpster. Seeing paint cans in the large container gave him a horrific idea. He emptied the cans of paint and paint remover over her inert form and with the lighter he carried everywhere, he set her afire. In moments the blaze was storming. He didn't know if the beating or the flames took her life.

He walked back to the lot where the crappy truck was parked and left for the shitty apartment. He was giddy at the thought of his first Asian victim. He didn't want to be thought a racist serial killer. Equal opportunity sounded better.

Part Two
Savannah

Chapter 10
Feeling The Heat

Bad Penny fell sleep with the shitty little black and white television built in the last century on. He saw flames in his dream and they warmed him to his core. When he woke the local news was on. Of course the tv only got one channel.

The lead story was about a burned body found in a dumpster downtown and the rash of murders in Atlanta. Although appearing to be unconnected, authorities now believed they were the work of a serial killer, the first in Atlanta since Wayne Williams was convicted for the heinous Atlanta child murders from '79-'81, and they were looking for a person of interest. The report described a man, mid thirties, five foot nine, one hundred thirty-five to one fifty-five pounds, with dark hair described by some to be short, others longish, with a sparse beard. Although that could describe thousands of men in Atlanta, it was worrisome. He didn't have much experience in Atlanta, that he could remember anyway, and even though he'd liked it so far, maybe it was time to relocate. Unable to remember much about Georgia, using his iPad and the Internet, pulled up Google Maps. He knew he had to take advantage of the device while he could since he didn't even know who his internet service provider was and he didn't have the checking account or credit card to pay the bill. Its days were numbered.

Summer approaching and thinking he would like the ocean, the warmer climate and the chicks wearing smaller, more revealing outfits, he targeted Savannah. Located on the Atlantic Ocean, Savannah was one of the nation's most important seaports. He packed his few possessions in the crappy truck and wasted no time leaving, without even letting Myriam know. He knew she'd notice and re-rent his room. As he drove too fast along the surface street, a dog, a mangy old cur, darted in front of his truck. Unable to stop in time he ran over the dog and knew immediately it was dead. He got out of the truck, picked up the dog and cradling it in his arms, carried him to the side of the street, and sat down and sobbed uncontrollably. He hurt like he'd never hurt before. After retrieving the tire tool from the back of his truck he gently carried the poor animal to a nearby vacant lot and with his newly gained strength from lifting weights took just a few minutes to dig a shallow resting spot. After placing him carefully in the excavation and covering him, he bowed his head and said a silent prayer, making the sign-of-the-cross after. A few minutes of mourning over the dead dog, and he gained a small bit of control over his emotions, so he could be on his way. Getting back in his truck, he made his way through downtown Atlanta and jumped on Interstate 75 and headed south.

Passing Turner Field, the home of baseball's Atlanta Braves, Bad Penny thought a hotdog with chopped onions, relish and mustard, and a beer would be good. He didn't think he'd ever had a hotdog before but he thought one sounded swell. A few miles south of town, looking in the rearview mirror he could see the discrete skylines of downtown and midtown and imagined north of them, the skylines of Buckhead and perimeter north. He wished the angle in the mirror were wide enough to see all four together. Atlanta's skyline wasn't one of the more famous ones in the US, but was very nice. About halfway to Macon, where he would pickup I-16e to Savannah, he stopped at a combination service station, convenience store and liquor store and bought a scratch-off lotto ticket, some cigarettes, a Mountain Dew and a bag of nacho cheese-flavored Doritos, the breakfast of champions. He won five dollars on the scratch off ticket. It paid for his meal. He noticed that the makers of snacks had started being honest in their nutrition labels, finally admitting what everyone else already knew—that there weren't three and a half servings in the small bag and that everyone would finish the bag and all the calories. The bastards—it was about time. Eating cheap because he was still trying to conserve his cash due to the fact that if he didn't regain his memory of who he was he wouldn't know the source of his money. Still nervous from hearing that the police were seeking a person of interest he chewed his fingernails the rest of the trip. Ironic, because in his previous life, of which he had no memory, he would spend a hundred dollars on mani/pedis every other week. As he drove he thought about the Atlanta Braves. It looked like they were destined for a mediocre season. He seemed to like baseball pretty well, but he was pretty sure he'd never been to a game before. He liked the statistics of baseball—era, rbi, batting average, on base percentage. He found it all to be mathematically interesting. The temperature was already warming as he drove further south from Atlanta.

It took about an hour and a quarter to reach Macon, a small city of almost one hundred thousand, seventy-five miles south of Atlanta. Bypassing the north end of town he thought maybe he wouldn't mind spending a little time there. A mix of a few nice taverns, fast food restaurants and hotels on the frontage road that would probably offer him good opportunities for his pastime.

A thought of the dog he hit earlier momentarily flashed through his mind and returned him to tears. He had to chase the thoughts away with, happier images, images of his Asian victim aflame, and that thought warmed him.

He took an unusual—at least in the south—left hand exit off of I-75 to pick up I-16 to Savannah. According to Mapquest it would take about two-and-a-half hours to get from Macon to Savannah. It didn't take that long to figure out it would be a very boring drive. The tall Georgia Pines encroached on both sides of the broad concrete ribbon, attempting to gain purchase. Power lines were held high in the air by giant steel-framed skeletons that looked like stick figures with outstretched arms. Not many exits and not much at the ones he did reach. The truck didn't have cruise control, so he had to be careful not to speed since he was *a person of interest.* The skin where his nascent tattoo resided itched as it healed. He hoped that by July maybe his spree might be over, the heat would be off and he could celebrate Independence Day by returning to Atlanta for a Braves game.

Chapter 11
Starting again

From what Bad Penny had seen on the internet, Savannah was one of the most historical towns in the country and had been voted by one reality tv ghost-hunting show as the spookiest town in America. Ghosts abounded in Savannah and he thought that might work to his advantage.

The trees shrouding the streets were draped with the Spanish moss for which Savannah was famous. As he pulled into town the first thing he recognized was Bonaventure Cemetery described in *Midnight in The Garden of Good and Evil*, the best selling true crime story by John Berendt. He didn't know how he knew it but it seemed to be buried in his core, his innate, knowledge.

Across the street from the cemetery to the south sat a five story pale green painted stucco apartment building. Bad Penny thought it looked like a possibility. Entering the building, it smelled like old people. He found the onsite management office. In luck—they had a furnished one bedroom available. An Art Deco building, the first floor had access to the balcony-like open second floor via a wide sweeping staircase. His new apartment was on the third floor and overlooked the beautiful park-like cemetery. He got his clothes inside and decided to go to a small liquor store he'd noticed next door to get some whiskey. He didn't know how long he'd be in Savannah, but in case he wanted to do some entertaining he needed some alcohol. The stronger, the better.

Penny went to the small liquor store nestled between one side of his new building and an alley on the other side, picked up a three liter bottle of Jack Daniels. Then decided to go into the Coffee Fox, across the broad street. Not a Starbucks like the yupsters prefer, the Coffee Fox had concrete floors, mismatched, sagging leather sofas and battered wood tables. His kind of place for a cup of strong, black, dark roast.

He sat near a pretty young woman with brown hair who seemed nervous, clasping her hands in front of her mouth, all of her fingers picking at the nails on the opposite hand and she looked like she'd been crying.

"Hi darling. Can I help?"

"Thank you. But no. I'm a writer, unpublished, but a writer, nonetheless. I have a twenty-five thousand word manuscript on my iPad and I left it somewhere. There's no way I can re-create the writing and I'm distraught. I wish someone would just kill me."

"Well, I might can help you with that."

"I beg your pardon."

"Bad joke, just kidding. Is there anything I can do to help?"

"Maybe. I had lunch yesterday at The Cotton Exchange, a pub on the wharf. They're known for Mean Jean's world famous bloody Marys, named for the bartender who's worked there for over twenty years. I've been going there for years. I shouldn't have had one. It seemed stronger than usual. Then later yesterday afternoon I noticed my tablet was missing. I may have left it there. I called and they didn't find it but I'd like to check for myself and I wouldn't mind you walking with me. It would calm me down." The Cotton Exchange was one of the many local bars and pubs famous for their apparitions. Legend was it had three or four playful spooks and one evil wraith.

"Happy to. Let's do it. I'm Penny, by the way."

"Thank you, I'm Anette."

They walked up Braughton to Bay St., which ran parallel to River Street, up above it and behind the inns, shops and taverns that fronted the river walk. Short underground historically significant tunnels connected the streets. As they started down the steep steps of a tunnel Penny placed his hand in the small of her back reassuringly, comfortingly and securely. It was a strong masculine gesture that made her feel safe. On the second step he shoved as hard as he could. Tumbling head over heels thirty feet to the bottom she came to a rest on the hundreds of years old stone landing with her leg twisted behind her and a large lump on her head.

Bad Penny rushed to her side and taking her head lovingly in his hands he blew her a kiss and twisted it violently, breaking her neck and killing her instantly. The erotic thrill he derived from her dying in his hands was electric. Then, fueled by the adrenalin rush, he bounded to the top of the stairs. He knew that like alcohol for some, drugs for others and sex for the addicted he would never be able to stop. Homicide was his drug, the sound of a neck breaking or a knife slicing open someone's throat, the warm, coppery smell of blood pouring from a wound, the horrified look in a victim's eyes—these were his drugs, what he needed and would continue to pursue, as life–giving as air, food or water, to Bad Penny. Emerging from the dark tunnel into the sunshine didn't warm him nearly as much as killing the young woman did.

Bad Penny went back to the apartment and, exhausted from his drive to Savannah and his first in-town killing, lay down on the green chenille sofa and napped. He dreamed of the eight murders he'd committed and was comforted by it, but he woke up chilled and crying and didn't know why. Recalling his last dream, he remembered the accidental running over of the dog. It haunted him still.

Napping until after twelve o'clock he wanted to see what, if anything, was going on in Savannah after midnight on a Tuesday. Went out and was surprised to see the sidewalks were teeming with tourists sightseeing and locals hitting the bars and pubs.

He noticed a club called Jazz'd, that had a flight of stairs descending from the sidewalk to its basement location. He thought it looked like a place he'd like but the sign on the door said it closed at midnight, so he made a mental note to come back and try again.

***

Bad Penny didn't expect to start a reign of terror his first day in town so he *intended* to lay low the next couple of days. But his intentions didn't bear out.

Returning to Jazz'd, the next night, he walked down the staircase to the doorway and entered the dark, dimly lit labyrinth. It gave off a cool vibe. He heard the sounds of a live jazz band from deeper in the club. The Smith Brothers, a clever name as the members consisted of two African-Americans, one caucasian and one hispanic gentleman.

Bad Penny thought to himself, *two god damn niggers and a fucking Mexican.* He thought the white lead singer playing rhythm guitar was pretty good, but he could have done without the others. But he also figured that if the white guy would be in a band with those others, that that told him all he needed to know about him. So he didn't like the white bastard either.

He sat at the bar, not really fitting in, looking the way he did, dressed in jeans, t-shirt and with his unkempt beard. The rest of the couples and singles in the half-full bar were dressed nicely, what could be described as dressy-casual. He ordered a jack on-the-rocks.

Two effeminate, well-dressed young men sat down a stool away from him. They giggled and drank cosmos looking altogether too gay. "Fucking fags," he said under his breath.

Not hearing what he said, the one nearer to him said, "Good evening," and raised his cosmopolitan glass with a nod of his head.

"How you doin?" Bad Penny responded.

"Oh, just splendid," was the lilting reply.

A short time later the bartender placed another jack on the bar in front of Bad Penny.

"I didn't order that," he protested weakly.

Nodding his head toward the guy who'd just spoken to him, the bartender said, "That gentleman bought it."

Bad Penny looked at the effete guy out of the corner of his eye without turning his head.

The effeminate man was grinning at him. Not really wanting to, but feeling like he should, he tilted the glass of warm amber liquid in his direction, in a gesture of thanks.

The guy attempted to draw Bad Penny into a conversation. But he wouldn't take the bait since he really didn't want to have to kill these guys since it seemed that he'd gotten away with the previous afternoon's murder. A news report said that it appeared that she'd died from an accidental fall down the three century-old steps. After another drink though, the guy asked him if he was interested in some good shit.

"What do you mean, good shit?" He'd gotten Penny's attention.

"You know, man, weed, chronic. We have some good shit in our car, just around the corner, in a parking lot."

Penny said, "That might be cool."

"Let me settle up then, and let's go. By the way, I'm Curtis. This is Wayne."

"Nice to meet you," Wayne said, the first time he'd spoken since they sat down.

"You too," said Bad Penny.

Settling their tabs, they were ready to leave. Walking out Curtis said, "Well like I said, we have some really good shit. You're gonna like it. We get it from a guy who buys it directly from the grower, in Florida.

Across the street, around the corner and two blocks down, their car was parked on the street. It belonged to Wayne, an Audi A6.

Wayne got in behind the wheel and Curtis held the door for Bad

Penny to get in the back seat, then taking him aback, climbed in beside him.

Wayne reached into the glove compartment and pulled out the bag of chronic. Passed it to Curtis who rolled a blunt. Taking a deep toke, he held it in and passed it to Bad Penny. Penny took the cigar-sized roll and inhaled deeply. "Yeah man, you were right. That's some real good shit.

They continued to pass it around as Wayne navigated the ethereal streets of the scariest town in America. After finishing the blunt, Curtis made his move. Reaching for the place between Penny's legs, in one smooth motion he pulled down the zipper and lowered his head into Penny's crotch. Penny wrapped his hands around Curtis' throat and tightened his grip. Curtis struggled, and kicking the back of the front seat, alerted Wayne to the life or death struggle. As Curtis' breath quickly ended and his strength ebbed, Wayne braked the car to a stop. Before he could turnaround though, with his ever-present knife, Bad Penny stabbed Curtis at the base of his neck, assuring his quick death, then, grabbing Wayne's head from the backseat and yanking it back, tore the knife through the front of his throat. The hot blood erupting from the deep gash in the front and side of his throat told Penny that Wayne's jugular had been severed and he wouldn't live more than a few seconds. When Wayne's head landed on the backseat floorboard between Bad Penny's feet, his eyes still moving in a neurological reaction, he knew he was right. The headless body slumped to the side in the front seat.

To the unattached head at his feet, still attempting to breathe, Bad Penny said, "Shut your goddamn mouth and die like a man. Cocksuckers," he said exiting the car. "You deserved to die."

After midnight in the spookiest city in America and Bad Penny had to walk back to his apartment alone. A series of nondescript city blocks lined with one- and two-story buildings. After a fifteen minute stroll all the while whistling past the graveyard, Bad Penny approached the bright neon of the historic Savannah Theatre. Erected in 1818, it was the oldest continuously operating theatre in America and one of Savannah's most haunted buildings. As he neared the building he heard the sound of a large crowd cheering and applauding. Checking the double glass doors just to be sure, he found them locked and at after 1:00 in the morning he knew the theatre shouldn't be open for business.

He had just heard the sounds of the mysterious ghost audience for which the theatre was famous. Getting the hell out of there, heart pounding, he ran as fast as he could back to his apartment. Shaken as he was by the ghost audience, he timidly looked under the bed, behind the sofa and in the closets, conflicted by being afraid of what he might find, and hoping beyond hope he wouldn't find haints or demons.

Falling asleep with the television on Bad Penny awakened to a news report saying that two men were found brutally murdered in their car and the police were describing it as a hate crime. Gay and lesbian groups would be up in arms pushing law enforcement to find the bigot who killed these poor men.

Bad Penny was giddy and emboldened by the news since it appeared attention would be directed away from him. He'd been able to commit three murders so far with little risk of being caught. And even though he seemed to be anti-Hispanic, anti-African American and anti-gay, he also murdered old men and hot women so he didn't consider himself a homophobe or racist. And he didn't have a pattern or a preferred victim so it would make it difficult for law enforcement to apprehend him. And although some might consider him insane, he knew what he was doing was wrong and the last thing he wanted was to end up as somebody's bitch in prison.

Penny decided to take a couple of days off from homicide and do some domestic chores. He called the building superintendent's office and asked, "Where's the goddamn washing machine?"

"Mind your language sir. There's no reason for talk like that. Second floor."

"Fuck you. I'm not going to be talked down to by a goddamn super. You will show me some fucking respect, goddammit." Then he hung up on the building employee.

He found a clothes washer and dryer on the second floor and after feeding them four dollars he got his jeans, t-shirts, socks and underwear washed and dried. He hated watching the machines run though, thinking it was a waste of time and that he could be doing something more important like scouting the city for more places to commit his special brand of horror. As he basked in the warmth of the washer and dryer and watched them spin, he daydreamed and thought he needed to make his killings more artistic and not just violent.

Finished with his washing, Penny had to find something to eat.

Remembering a truck stop a couple of exits west on I-16, the decision was made. The food wouldn't be bad. It was cheap and lots of truckers ate at them, so it had to be decent. And it'd be filling. So, he got in his crappy truck, headed toward the sun on 16 and fifteen minutes later he was sitting down to meat loaf, mashed potatoes and green beans with a big hunk of cornbread. And a huge glass of sweet tea. He looked down on yuppies and their obsession with having their wine with dinner. Everybody knew sweet tea was the house wine of the south. If you drank wine you were just showing off. What he didn't remember was that he used to be the worst kind of wine snob. Thinking while waiting for his food he decided he needed to find another gym and start working out again. He was making good progress and he needed to continue.

Sitting in the adjacent booth to the front of him, there was a couple, probably on a road trip, a family vacation, with a child, a little boy about three years old with blonde hair and blue eyes. The toddler was standing on the seat next to his mom, looking at Penny over the top of the seat. Penny thought he was cute, winked at him, and said, "Hi sport." The child ducked down below the seat back, embarrassed. Penny thought that he might like to have a kid some day. He was sure he'd be a good father.

***

The weekend's arrival brought with it a return of the need, the need to satisfy the urge that now consumed him like someone else might be addicted to cocaine or heroin.

Waiting until dark on Friday evening to go out, Bad Penny cut through the park across the street, one of the many downtown area parks and cemeteries for which Savannah was known. Most of them filled with statues commemorating the lives of civil war heroes, politicians, Savannah literary figures and musicians of note and others portraying angels and religious figures. A large park that would take over ten minutes to traverse, even via it's most direct route cutting through the middle. Arriving at the very center, the darkness was at its deepest and made him realize that he was afraid of this city, its ethereal denizens and its dark depths, where someone or some thing, like himself, might lurk waiting to strike.

From behind a large statue of a confederate soldier on a horse, he heard something, but it wasn't a sound to fear. He heard the sounds of passion. Peeking around the large base on which the horse was mounted he saw a couple having sex on a blanket.

The young woman was sitting on top of her lover with her back to Bad Penny. Slipping his knife from behind his back, he saw an opportunity and moved as fast as lightening. Grabbing her hair, pulling her head back and slicing her throat from behind, her head fell to the rear and was barely hanging on by a short strap of skin. Her body fell backwards. Using both of his hands he then plunged the butcher knife deep into the male's chest. The shock on his face gave Bad Penny the biggest thrill he'd had yet. The last thing the male saw in this life was his lover's head fall from her body after Bad Penny killed her, and then he experienced his own horrific death. And, confident that he wouldn't be suspected in any of the killings and unworried about DNA evidence since nobody knew who he was, Bad Penny then used his hand on himself to relieve the urge in his loins over both of the bodies.

Pleased with himself, he would make it an early evening. Five murders in four days. He was motivated to raise his kill numbers but he could relax the rest of the evening. He now had a goal to become the nation's all time most prolific serial killer. He would have to do some research to find out what that number would need to be.

Back at the apartment, Penny poured three fingers of Jack Daniels over ice in a cheap tumbler and settled down on the ugly green sofa to see what he could find on tv. Turning directly to the late night movie channels, he was in luck. *Silence of The Lambs* with the inimitable Sir Anthony Hopkins as the killer without a conscience, followed by *Psycho*, the great Alfred Hitchcock thriller. Before dawn, *American Psycho* starring Christian Bale would end at daylight. Who knew, might be that he'd be able to improve his technique with a knife by paying particular attention to the infamous shower scene in *Psycho*. It seemed that stabbing and slashing were becoming his favorite methods of mayhem. Refilling his glass and with the movies holding his interest, he was able to stay mostly awake until five-thirty a.m. Eventually he nodded off on the couch and later, came to in the middle of *American Psycho*. Getting up, he turned off the television, and trod heavily to the bathroom to get ready for bed. As he walked, he heard a voice call his name. Penny, Penny, we're watching and we won't let you get away with this.

He attributed hearing the voice to the Jack Daniels, but in the quiet of the early morning, turning the television back on to provide background noise and to help calm his frazzled nerves seemed like a good idea. Maybe coming to the most spectral city in America wasn't one of his better ideas. He seemed to be more on edge with each day that passed.

***

Waking late on Saturday morning he thought he'd check out a gym he'd noticed a couple of days before. He needed to get back into lifting and get serious about it. His hair was getting pretty long and his tat had healed and looked good. He needed to build some serious muscle now. He had a need to enhance the tough guy image he coveted.

He entered The Iron Palace with a swagger. Better than the first time he entered a gym three weeks earlier. Amazing what putting on a little muscle and killing a dozen people did for your self image. It was a serious gym. Not a machine to be found—barbells, dumbbells and kettle bells were scattered on the floor like a steel garden.

"How ya doin?" the guy sweeping the floor asked.

"Aiiight. You?"

"Okay. What can I do you for?"

"Want to join a gym."

"You've come to the right place. Best one in town."

"Yeah? Whatcha got?"

"Barbells, dumbbells, flat benches, inclined, declined, smith machine, squat racks, kettle bells. All your basics."

"Sounds like it'll work. Let's do it."

"Sounds good, let me get the paperwork. Haven't seen you around before."

"I haven't been around before. Visited here when I was in the Navy, decided to come back. I like all the hot chicks."

"I hear you. Savannah's got 'em."

Looking around the large space he could see that he had as much muscle as anybody there and with some work and just a little time he would be bigger and more muscular than the average weight lifter. He definitely was starting to look like a tough guy. He needed another large tattoo on his left arm, to match the one on the right. Then he would get more respect.

He got signed up and decided since he was there that he might as well get in a workout. Work biceps, the muscle most guys call the chick muscle because they believed women notice and like a sleeve stretching pair of upper arms. And it was Saturday, so getting a pump for Saturday night would be good.

Chapter 12
Making The Connection

'I don't know. I just think it's just too much of a coincidence, and with the seven murders in The Atl—well, it's not that far away you know," homicide detective Jordan Lynch said. Lynch was late thirties, attractive, with brunette hair and had been told she had more than a passing resemblance to Angelina Jolie. Married to the job, when people told her that, she always said she wished she were married to Brad Pitt.

"So, you think they're connected?" her partner, detective Roy Richardson said. "And connected to the ones in Atlanta?"

"Five deaths in less than a week? And seven in Atlanta? Yeah, that's too much. You know how I feel about coincidences. And you know, something about Anette Hartman's death, I just don't think she fell. "

"You think she was helped?"

"I'm leaning that way."

"So what do you want to do?"

"I think a little undercover work, an innocent tourist, alone, would be in order. It's Saturday night, you know.

***

Bad Penny searched the internet and decided on The Cotton Exchange, the restaurant and pub that his victim, Anette, had mentioned. Looked like a place that tourists and locals alike frequented. Deciding to make a night of it, he left early, about seven; in mid-spring there was still about an hour and a quarter before sunset with dark approaching rapidly after.

Walking down River Street with a spring in his step, Bad Penny was pumped. He felt like he was on his way to becoming one of America's most prolific serial killers of all time.

***

Detective Jordan Lynch sat on the low concrete seawall that ran along the waterway at the middle of River Street observing the throngs of people on the sidewalks. She wore trendy colorful summer clothing from the nearby Ralph Lauren Outlet store and carried shopping bags from the local shops. Tourists and locals blended together. She didn't know what she was looking for, but she hoped she'd know it when she saw it, based on her powers of intuition, honed by over fifteen years on the job.

Detective Richardson, the man she trusted more than any other except her dad, was on the other end of the street, in panhandler disguise.

***

The Cotton Exchange was at almost the mid-point of the length of River Street. The waterfront area that was now the street was where Savannah began. James Edward Oglethorpe, the founder, established the town here because the bluffs at this spot provided the best point from which to defend the nascent town from the Spanish in Florida. The first buildings, typically used as warehouses to store goods in the infant seaport town were built from lumber, starting in the 1730's, but because of the highly flammable nature of the cotton, lumber and rice being stored, beginning in the 1820's the structures and River Street itself began being reconstructed using ballast stone, it used by the high-masted, incoming ships to counterbalance their weight as they offloaded their goods.

Prior to the 1970's the bars along River Street catered mostly to sailors. But after The Cotton Exchange opened in 1971, the whole River Street area became a more family-friendly environment with restaurants, shops and attractions suitable for everyone.

Bad Penny entered The Cotton Exchange and chose a seat at the bar that was directly in front of the entry. The original to the 1730's building, uneven, wide-plank, wood floors made it a little challenging for Penny to walk due to his slight limp, the cause of which he had no memory. The walls made of the ballast stone during the 1820's. Except for two small windows looking out on River Street, the bar was quite dark, even in daylight.

On this evening, bartender *Mean* Jean, maker of the famed Cotton Exchange Bloody Mary was regaling bar patrons with stories of things flying untouched off of shelves, a radio turning itself on and cold coffee makers, unswitched on, brewing coffee. She herself having a steel ice scoop flung at her when she was alone in the bar.

Penny ordered a Jack on the rocks with a beer chaser. You could tell which ones were tourists since it was mostly them who asked servers to take pictures of them with their iPhones, everyone enjoying their Saturday night.

***

Detective Lynch felt that something wasn't right. She couldn't put her finger on it, but she felt very cold and goosies ran up and down her spine. She called her partner:

"It's me."

"Anything out of the ordinary?" He was on alert.

"Nothing. I'm just getting a weird feeling. Don't know what it is, but I feel something."

"Well, you know I trust your instincts as much as mine, so keep your eyes and ears open and be careful."

"You too."

***

Bad Penny strutted to the restroom, showing off his new muscles and in his plain white tee shirt, a good pump from his bicep workout earlier that day and his arm-covering tattoo. He could see looks of intimidation on the faces of men and looks of approval from women who liked the bad boy look.

Returning to his seat at the bar, he ordered another Jack with a beer back. Soon, two men started to get loud. Arguing over the girl of one that the other eyed too enthusiastically. The first picked up a beer mug and hurled it at he second. It bounced off his shoulder leaving him uninjured. The carom, arced above the bar and struck Bad Penny on the bridge of his nose. A bone-deep gash started blood flowing, that quickly covered his face. Silently, swiftly, the always-lurking, just under-the-surface Bad Penny emerged and blitzed to the other end of the bar and without saying a word unleashed a barrage of punches to the face of the one that threw the mug. Leaving him collapsed on the bar with more blood covering him than Penny had, he then turned his attention to the other guy and thinking if he hadn't started it by ogling the first one's girlfriend, he wouldn't have to do this and after an array of punches, elbows and head butts, left this guy in even worse condition than the first.

Penny returned to the restroom, this time to wash the blood from his face. The sink was full of red stained water from the massive amount of blood he'd lost from the gash on his nose.

Looking in the mirror, he thought his face didn't look that bad, in fact the scar between his eyes that was sure to form, would enhance the tough guy look he coveted. His white tee however, was done, the top half of which was stained dark reddish-brown from the blood that had poured down his face.

His Saturday night was over. He needed to get out of there before the police he was sure someone had called, arrived.

**

Detective Lynch heard on her department issued earbud that there was a disturbance at the Cotton Exchange.

"Roy, did you hear that?"

"Affirmative."

"I'm responding."

"Negative. Jordan, I'll be there in three minutes. Do not go in without me. Got it? Do you copy?"

"Yeah, yeah, I copy."

Waiting for Detective Richardson she took pictures of the crowded sidewalks with her iPhone. If backup didn't get there in time maybe she'd get a shot of someone relevant. After rapidly snapping a dozen photos of the throngs, Richardson showed up and they crossed the street together toward The Cotton Exchange.

**

"Detectives Lynch and Richardson," she said, badging the manager who was trying to settle everyone down.

The woman-in-charge explained about the two guys having an argument and when one threw a beer mug hitting a third guy, the third one kicked both of their asses. Then, after cleaning up in the bathroom, he made a hasty exit. They'd missed him by a minute.

They got the victims contact info—they were in too much pain to answer questions and needed to get to the hospital—interviewed witnesses and decided to call it a night.

The detectives walked to their cars parked on Bay Street, on the bluff above River.

"So I'll see you in the morning?" She was anxious to look at the pictures she'd taken on a large screen, see if they turned up anything.

Even on a Sunday morning.

"Yeah. I'll see you at the office in the a.m."

***

Richardson stopped for bagels on the way in. Wanted to do his share for the office. Not leave the task for any of the women. It wasn't just a chick's job. Passing out the bagels, he gave Jordan a poppyseed one, he knew she liked. Held onto an everything bagel for himself, and gave the rest, whole grain, garlic and plain to the admin staff that was keeping the place running on a Sunday morning.

"So what'cha got?" he asked.

"Just downloaded the pics from my iPhone to the laptop. You can look with me." They had a dozen pictures of the crowds on the sidewalk that needed to be examined.

They struck gold on the fifth picture. A male, bearded and tats, weightlifter, his tee shirt soaked in what looked like blood in a photo among a large crowd. "Can you focus on him, blow him up, torso and face?"

"Only in seconds, duh," she said. She knew her partner was not technologically astute and she liked busting his balls about it.

"Great, we can get him for assault."

"I don't know. I'm getting a feeling. Something about him just doesn't feel right. Remember those homicide guys in ATL, working the murders, we read about? The report said they had a person of interest. Let's send them this picture, see if we get lucky."

"Sounds good."

***

Bad Penny woke up early on Sunday morning—lay in bed rubbing his hands. His knuckles were cut and bruised and his hands swollen from the beating he gave the two guys. He felt great about it though. The pain made him feel alive and energized.

He went to the bathroom, peed and brushed his teeth, then went to the small kitchen and started coffee brewing. The rhythmic sound of the coffee percolating provided a counterpoint to the sound of the archaic window unit air conditioner. While the coffee was brewing he did a hundred pushups and a hundred bodyweight squats. He continued to get stronger and bigger as he put on more muscle.

***

Detective Townsend cooked his twelve-year-old daughter, Samrya breakfast like he did every morning. Scrambled eggs, turkey bacon and buttered whole grain toast with cherry preserves. She staggered downstairs rubbing her eyes with balled up fists.

"Morning, daddy."

"Good morning, sweetheart. How's my baby?"

"I'm fine. Sleepy"

"What time did you turn out your light?"

"Eleven."

"Well, that's why."

"But daddy, I have that math test. I've just got to get an "A"."

"That's my girl. Get good marks and you won't have to be a cop like your old man. You can be a prosecutor, or even a judge."

"Aw, daddy, but I want to be a detective like you. You're the best."

"Eat your breakfast, sweetie. We have time to talk about it before you have to make that decision."

Detective Townsend enjoyed the time he spent with Samyra everyday eating breakfast together and driving her to John F. Kennedy Middle School. Since his wife had left them they'd grown closer and he thought this was a big reason for it. Getting involved in her life. And knowing what was going on.

"Have a good day, sweetheart," he said, leaning over to kiss her.

"You too, daddy. Be careful, love you."

"I will. I love you too, sweetheart." If they'd witnessed it perps wouldn't believe tough-guy Townsend was Mr. Mom, but he wouldn't have it any other way.

He parked his unmarked Crown Victoria, commonly known among law enforcement as a CVPI—the abbreviation for Crown Vic Police Interceptor—in the headquarters parking lot. Even though the car was being replaced by the smaller Taurus at police departments nationwide, Townsend resisted his bosses trying to force him to change because he liked the larger, more powerful engine and the larger cabin.

He seemed too happy for a Monday morning greeting everyone warmly. Usually a term reserved for a blonde-haired surfer dude and not an African-American, Townsend was known as the golden boy for his success in felony arrests and his squeaky clean presence. He smelled the coffee someone else had started brewing but brought up his email before he even got his first cup, saw an email from the Savannah, GA Police department, a Detective Jordan Lynch. She asked him to look at a picture and see if he recognized the man.

He opened the attachment and waited for it to download. The guy looked familiar, but not exact, a full beard, more muscles than he imagined in his mind. He couldn't picture a tattoo in his mind's eye either. But still, *think*, he thought to himself.

"Hot damn! Wentworth."

"Nick, you've got to see this," he yelled across the room.

"What have I got to see," He called back.

"Just get over here."

"You know those murders we saw in the news in Savannah?"

"Yeah, yeah, yeah."

The detective on the investigation sent me a picture, taken on a sidewalk." He pulled up the picture. "Tell me who this is."

"Wentworth!"

"Bingo."

"Is there a phone number?" Ramsey said, excited.

"Yep."

"Let's call her, then."

***

"Detective Lynch."

"Detective Lynch, this is Detectives Townsend and Ramsey, Atlanta."

"Thanks for calling. Do you know my boy?"

"You bet we do. Name's Pennington Wentworth the 2nd. Why don't you tell us what you got?"

Detective Lynch explained about the bar fight and with the picture of him with blood on his shirt and witness' descriptions, that this Wentworth was her prime suspect. They told her of their interview with him about the first murder and that they'd dismissed him as a suspect but witnesses put someone matching his description at the scene of all their murders. He'd disappeared, appeared to have vanished, and now, with him showing up in Savannah, at the sight of more murders, he'd just jumped to number one with a bullet, on their hit list.

"Why don't y'all come on down? Let's find this guy, lock him up."

"Sounds like a plan. I think we have some travel dollars. Let us okay it with the boss, the Chief of Detectives."

After exchanging good-byes Ramsey said, "Looks like a road trip is in order."

"Sounds like it," said Townsend. "Let's see what the boss says then I'll have to see if Samyra can stay with the neighbors two or three days."

They knocked on the Chief of Detectives' open door. Jim Hester's office walls were plastered with team pennants and pictures of various Atlanta Braves and Falcons players. He'd been a linebacker on his high school football team and always told himself and anyone who would listen that he could have advanced further if he'd only had the chance. On his credenza sat a small replica of the Dale Earnhardt no. 3 car.

"Yeah, what is it?"

Townsend started as they entered his office. "Boss, you know Savannah has had some murders?"

"Yeah, what's that got to do with us?"

Sitting down in front of the chief's desk, a Chipper Jones Bobblehead doll, that somehow unnerved him, faced Ramsey, *grown men playing with dolls,* he thought.

"One of their detectives sent us a picture of a possible and guess who it is."

"I don't want to guess. Tell me."

Remember our person of interest—Wentworth?"

"Yeah, what about him?'

"It's his picture. He's grown a beard, got some tats, built himself up, but it's him."

It didn't take him long to connect the dots. "Well, go get yourselves a killer."

"Thanks boss. That's what we hoped you'd say."

Townsend had to call his next-door-neighbor to find out if Samyra could stay with them. They had a daughter a year older than her, and they'd become good friends since his wife left them when she needed a good friend.

The only thing Ramsey had to do was let the bartenders at Marlowe's, his favorite neighborhood watering hole, know that he'd be gone a couple of days or else they'd wonder if something was wrong.

Chapter 13
Track down

Townsend drove and picked up his partner at the apartment complex in which he'd lived alone since his divorce six years earlier. Ramsey'd admitted he'd had an affair with a secretary on the job and she wouldn't even discuss it with him other than to say, I hate cheaters, and walk out.

To Townsend it felt like he was going on a spring break road trip during college, especially since he was going south on I-75 toward Florida and it's sunshine and powder-white beaches.

A mile before the Hudson Bridge exit they saw a sign for Starbucks. Much better than the coffee they'd had at the office, they agreed they should stop.

At the drive thru window Ramsey got a venti sumatra black and Townsend ordered an iced grande cinnamon dolce latte. A CVS Pharmacy was across the street and Ramsey needed a bandage to cover the spot where he'd nicked himself shaving earlier. Townsend waited in the car and sipped his iced latte while Ramsey went inside. He returned five minutes later and adjusted Townsend's rearview mirror so he could see to position the small round bandage.

Ramsey, always the smartass said, "What does a brother do when he cuts himself and doesn't want to wear a "flesh" colored bandage?"

"Come on man. They have brown ones. Don't be racist."

"Hey, I didn't know. I'm glad they do. I was worried about you. I didn't want you to have to wear the wrong color.

"So, you were just looking out for my best interests?"

"That's it, brother. I got your back."

"I'm glad that you do." With a smirk.

The early morning sun hitting the trees cast shadows that extended to cover almost all lanes in both directions of the interstate.

Three quarters of an hour later they made Macon. Townsend said, "I used to date a chick from Macon when I was in college. Wow. She was wild! A tiger in the sack."

Said Ramsey, "TMI, brother. The only thing I know about Macon is it's where the Allman Brothers used to live and where Duane Allman was killed on his motorcycle. Damn shame, the band was never the same after that. They should have made a lot more music. Southern rock and roll. I know they have an Allman Brothers museum here, somewhere. In the house they lived in. I should to go visit it sometime. You should come with me."

"Tell you what, let's don't and say we did. The only reason you white guys listen to rock and roll is you can't dance. If you could, you'd listen to soul music or hip hop."

"Yeah, yeah, yeah. Who says I can't dance? I can dance."

Upon reaching downtown Macon, they picked up I-16E, an unusual left hand exit toward Savannah and less than an hour later they were passing Dublin, GA, famous for its month long St. Patrick's celebration, an homage to its Irish namesake.

Ramsey cracked his window and flicking open a silver Zippo lighter, put fire to a cigarette.

"How much further is it, daddy?" he said.

"We've got a little over an hour left, sweetheart. Why don't you take a nap?"

He stubbed out the cigarette in the ashtray after one drag, and said, "That's a good idea. I'll grab forty winks. I didn't need that cigarette anyway."

Curled up against the window, he stared at the passing landscape for five whole minutes before he was snoring.

As they neared Savannah, Townsend entered the 201 Habersham St. address in Apple Maps on his iPad and less than a third of an hour later pulled up in front of the three-story brick building, home to the Savannah-Chatham Metropolitan Police. With its beginnings in the 1790's the building was the oldest continually serving police headquarters in the U.S.

Entering the green canopied glass door, they badged the desk officer and asked for Detective Lynch. A moment later she hurried down the broad staircase.

"Detective, good to meet you," Ramsey said.

"Call me Jordan. You too."

"All right then, Jordan," said Townsend.

"Come on up."

She bounded up the stairs to the third floor, her long brunette hair tied back in a ponytail swinging from side-to-side, looking much younger than her thirty-eight years. Stiff from their nearly four hour drive, they followed slowly. As they sat down around her desk, Ramsey said, "Nice digs."

"Thanks. It's home."

Ramsey wandered over to a window overlooking a beautiful green space, one of Savannah's large parks decorated with huge trees draped in Spanish moss. He clipped his nails over a trash can.

"So where do we start?" Townsend asked.

"Old fashioned beat cop work, canvasing hotels, apartments?"

"Sounds good."

"He met several of his victims in bars," Ramsey reminded.

Townsend: "Good idea. When the sun goes down we can start staking out the watering holes."

Jordan said, "Let me talk to the boss. I'm sure he'll get us some more cops, go undercover."

"Good idea. Wentworth knows us. So we can't be lead. Did he see you?"

"I don't see how. I was a hundred feet away, across the street, on a crowded sidewalk. Taking pictures, no different than any other tourist."

"You should be lead, then." Ramsey liked her. Her competence and experience showed themselves in her every movement and every uttered word.

"Give me a minute. I'll go check with the boss."

Townsend: "We're not going anywhere."

***

Exiting his apartment, his next door neighbor, a blue-haired elderly woman in her eighties, opened the door to her apartment at the same time.

"'"Was that your tv playing so loudly, a couple of nights ago, young man?"

"I don't know. Did you ask your other neighbors?"

"I've lived here for over forty years. I've been a single lady the whole time. It's always been a nice, quiet building. If it was you don't make me call the super."

"Call the goddamn super, lady, and you'll regret it."

"Oh dear."

You're goddamn right, oh dear…now, have a nice day."

***

Bad Penny went to the gym. The place was almost empty on a Monday morning. He was glad for that. He didn't want to have to deal with any assholes.

He got a good workout in, doing bench press, front squat, shoulder press and barbell rows.

Noticing a heavy bag in the corner, he thought he should start punching the bag, but with his hands still sore from the beating he gave the two assholes he figured he should wait a couple of days.

***

"The boss said no problem. Just catch us a serial killer," Said Jordan when she returned.

"That's the plan," said Townsend, "I have a reputation to maintain." He wasn't arrogant, but he was proud of his stature as the department's golden boy and he wanted to keep his record unblemished.

The chief called a meeting and Jordan led it and would be the lead on this investigation. Richardson watched proudly since they both considered her his protégée and him her mentor.

She was in control and spoke to the roughly forty officers in the room. "Okay, listen up people. These men are detectives Anthony Townsend and Nick Ramsey from Atlanta. It looks like we've got a serial killer in our midst. They'll tell you what they know. After that I'll fill in any blanks. Then we'll answer questions."

Lynch's iPad was connected to an overhead projector and the picture of Pennington Wentworth II in the bloody tee-shirt appeared on a five foot screen. Townsend and Ramsey explained the situation, that they'd had seven homicides in metropolitan Atlanta, at first appearing to be unrelated, but after interviews with people that had contact with the victims, that there had been a male, white, mid-thirties that had been with, or at least near, each victim shortly before their murders which led them back to considering a person of interest they'd interviewed after the first. Detective Lynch had taken a picture of the person they'd interviewed and now they felt like the twelve deaths in two cities were related and attributed to the male they'd interviewed after the first homicide.

Detective Lynch took over. "Okay people, this is our boy on the screen. I took his picture Saturday night. He's used a two by four, a knife, his bare hands, a necktie and in the case of a monsignor, a solid gold chalice, to murder his victims. We have no reason to think he has a gun, but no reason to believe he doesn't."

Jordan remembered the one time she was in a gunfight. Her first year as a detective, a man took his wife and two daughters hostage in their home, threatening to kill them and himself. First on the scene, she'd gotten an opening and taken him out. She hadn't liked it but she did her job well, but at the same time hoped she'd never have to do it again. It had taken a year of talking to the department shrink to get it out of her head.

"Any questions? No? Two man teams checking all hotels, motels and apartments downtown first. We have copies of the picture for all of you. Pick them up on the way out. We have a grid staked out, we'll work it north from the river. Guessing he'd want to be where the action is and not one of the islands. We hope not, anyway. Me and Detectives Townsend and Ramsey will be in the car, floating. Radio if you get anything and we'll get there as quick as we can. Stay alert and be careful out there."

Lynch, Townsend and Ramsey changed into casual clothes and sneakers, didn't want to look like cops and had to be able to give chase if need be.

The day ended without luck. No one at any of the apartments or hotels they visited recognized Pennington Wentworth II from the photo. It would have been an unbelievable stroke of good luck to find him on the first day, anyway.

***

Bad Penny decided not to go out on Monday night.

Settling down on the ugly old sofa with three fingers of bourbon, in front of a tv with a minuscule screen and only two channels, he found an Atlanta Braves game. He realized he knew nothing about baseball and didn't know why, but he thought the atmosphere was exciting.

During commercials Bad Penny would do sets of fifty pushups. Before the game was over he'd knocked out five hundred. The good thing about him being so thin when he started working out was the muscles in his upper body were getting thick and full with the veins popping out. His chest, shoulders and triceps were pumped and growing before his eyes when he got in bed about midnight.

***

Staking out several of the bars on River Street, the task force communicated by radio. A couple of times they observed men that looked enough like Wentworth to put them on edge, but Townsend and Ramsey immediately knew when they arrived on the scenes that it wasn't their man.

After the second false alarm Detective Lynch told everyone over the radio, "No worries, people. Stay on your toes. We'd rather be wrong than miss him, so if you have a possible let us know."

At midnight on a Monday they decided he wasn't going to show.

"Okay folks, let's call it a night. See you bright and early in the morning. Show up on time and come dressed to play." She and Richardson headed back to the house.

***

Lynch, Townsend and Ramsey were at the office early, coffee and donuts ready for the arriving troops.

Everyone was there by eight. Cops and donuts went together like pretzels and beer and five dozen plain, jelly-filled and chocolate ones had disappeared in less than fifteen minutes. Nothing but boxes of crumbs and chocolate- and jelly-smears remained.

"Okay, ladies and gentlemen, let's do it. These printouts have the updated list of city blocks we want you to start on this morning. Get out there and find our boy.

***

Bad Penny left early Tuesday morning. Decided to try a Starbucks he'd seen, for a change. He wasn't looking for a target, but he was a killer of opportunity. If one presented him- or herself he would take advantage of it.

"I'll have a large," he refused to say *venti*, "dark roast, black." If you ordered a venti choco, frappe, mocha, whatever, you were just a preppie asshole. After a refill, he'd had enough of yuppiedom. It was 11 o'clock and he needed one more accessory to compliment his tats and new muscles. By god, I'll get my fucking ears pierced. Then I'll get some goddamn respect.

A tattoo parlor in the next block had a sign in its window advertising piercings. The parlor was large, and a latino tattoo artist and piercer by the name of Shane said he could help Bad Penny with piercings. Bad Penny picked out temporary star-shaped earrings and Shane got another latino employee, Juan, to assist. Both piercers stood on each side of Bad Penny and, on the count of three, they fired the piercing guns at the same time. Shane said, "That was just in case you felt queasy and wanted to back out after the first one."

"Come on, man. You think a little thing like that would bother me?" In fact the sound and feel of his own cartilage being pierced made Bad Penny's stomach churn.

***

The number of hotels and apartments made the job tedious. Although a small city, being a resort town, Savannah had an unusually high number of each, for it's size. The officers doing the canvas approached the task seriously. They knew that if they found Wentworth, it would enhance the golden boy's rep and they would be solving murders, but more importantly now, preventing more.

For the second day they didn't find his home base, so they continued into the evening to hit the bars and taverns again.

At 7:00 pm, two of the undercover cops, Waits and Stefanelli, male and female officers pretending to be on a date, entered and staked out Pour Larry's, known for the presence of its resident evil spirit. Lesser hauntings included finding whiskey glasses broken on the bar when employees arrived to work in the morning, bottles being flung at workers and the distinct smell of burnt human flesh. As it turns out, the building was built in 1855 by a John Montmollon who Was a slave trader and made his fortune in the horrific capture, transport and sale of other human beings. However, Karma got its revenge, as he died in a fire aboard a steamship on the Savannah River, hence the sickly-sweet smell of burnt human flesh that permeated the walls and floor of Pour Larry's. On this night though, the undercover cops were unconcerned with evil spirits, but instead with an evil human, in the form of a serial killer.

***

Bad Penny readied himself to mingle with the tourists on a Tuesday night. Explaining that he was new in town and asking the advice of a barista at Starbucks that morning, she'd recommended Pour Larry's, a local watering hole frequented by tourists and locals alike.

Knowing he was a bad ass and looking the part, Bad Penny strutted down West St. Julian Street, reminiscent of John Travolta strutting down the sidewalk in the movie, Saturday Night Fever.

He entered Pour Larry's around eight o'clock. Said to the bartender, "Give me a god damn whiskey with a beer back."

The cops on stakeout recognized him immediately.

Waits lifted the lapel of his sport coat and spoke into the tiny radio mike pinned to the underside.

"The suspect is here. Repeat, suspect is here."

Detective Lynch responded, "K, got it. The cavalry is on its way."

"He just showed. Let's roll," she said to the ATL detectives.

"Right on," said Townsend.

"Let's get him." Ramsey urged.

Six patrol cars plus the one carrying Lynch, Ramsey and Townsend converged swiftly, sans sirens, on Pour Larry's. That made fifteen police plus the two in the bar to take down Pennington Wentworth II.

"What's your 20?" Waits asked into his lapel mike.

"Just pulled up, on our way in. Where is he?" Lynch.

"In the front door, right side of the bar."

"K."

Ramsey, Townsend and Lynch entered first, with twelve cops behind them.

Taking no chances, all three drew their weapons and trained them on the suspect.

Adrenalin working, Lynch shouted at the top of her lungs. "Wentworth, hands on the bar. Now."

"You talkin' to me?" Bad Penny said.

"Wentworth, on the floor!" Ramsey yelled.

Although like all criminals, he would have played the role of the innocent anyway. "Who's Wentworth?" Bad Penny said. "Dude, what's this all about? What's the problem? You must have me confused with someone else. But I'll be happy to help if I can."

Townsend approached him and went up side his head with his Beretta 9mm, knocking him to the floor.

Seventeen officers with weapons drawn caused quite a commotion and if they could tell it, probably frightened the evil spirits that called Pour Larry's home.

After checking him for weapons and finding the large knife he now carried everywhere, he flipped it to Ramsey. Pinning his hands behind his back and cuffing him, Townsend shouted, "You're under arrest for multiple murders."

Playing the role, he still protested. "Murders? What in the world are you talking about?

"Don't play dumb, Wentworth. You remember us."

"Remember you? I've never seen you before in my life, but if I can help you I will. And who's this Wentworth?" Bad Penny couldn't remember them since his damaged brain had lost all recollection of the Pennington Wentworth, II era.

Townsend and Ramsey pulled him to his feet and through the gauntlet of officers, dragged him to their car.

Chapter 14
Wrap Up

After getting Wentworth booked and into a cell in the Chatham County jail the night before, they got him processed first thing this morning. The jail held over thirteen hundred prisoners, making it one of the largest and busiest county jails in the state of Georgia. Paperwork was the worst part of police work. He had to be processed in Savannah even though everyone knew what was as yet, unspoken. Atlanta would get first shot at him.

The detectives were rehashing what had happened over coffee.

"Can you believe that guy? Acting like he didn't remember us," Ramsey said.

"Yeah, sure he didn't. He remembers us. He was just doing what all criminals and cons do, maintaining their innocence no matter how hopeless the situation. They all do it." Townsend agreed.

"I don't know. I hate to think about it getting him off, but I think there might be something wrong with him. It seems like he has a mental problem." Lynch offered.

"Anyone who can kill twelve people has a mental problem, but if he knew the difference in right and wrong he'll be convicted anyway. Pass me another one of those asiago garlic bagels?" Said Ramsey as he helped himself to another spoonful of cream cheese.

"Careful, partner, better watch that waistline." Said Townsend.

"You better watch it big boy, you aren't my momma. You take care of your waistline and I'll take care of mine."

Said Det. Lynch, "I guess we should get him ready for the move to the ATL."

"I'll call the chief of d's and he'll get us a transport with some uniforms. We don't want to take any chances with this guy. Too high profile. If anything were to go wrong newspapers and television in both cities would fry us." Ramsey.

"I don't even want to think about it." Lynch shuddered.

After spending several hours working out the details at the departments in both Atlanta and Savannah they had arranged for Wentworth to be moved the following day. A transport vehicle would arrive before noon.

***

"I have an idea," Lynch said. Your last night in town. Let's go out for dinner.

"Great idea," said Ramsey.

"Yeah, let's do it," echoed Townsend.

"Where do you want to go?" she asked.

"Anywhere that has good seafood," said Townsend.

"That's only every restaurant in town. Trust me. I'll pick a good one. A local haunt. Literally."

"Thanks for warning me," said Ramsey. "I'll be packing."

"It's almost five. Why don't we go back to our hotel and get cleaned up, change clothes." Townsend said.

"Sounds good. I'll pick y'all up…say 6:30?

"We'll be waiting." Ramsey was already hungry.

***

Townsend and Ramsey were staying at the Hilton Garden Inn on West Bay Street just a block from the river front. After getting a shower and changing they went to the hotel bar for a beer while they waited for Jordan. Ramsey had a Bud Light and Townsend a Terrapin Mosaic, a tasty microbrew made in Athens, GA. Through the large picture window looking out onto Bay Street they saw Jordan when she pulled up and parked in the fire zone, out front. One of the perks of being a cop. They met her on the sidewalk.

Jordan was dressed in a stylish but affordable print dress from Forever 21. Dressing well on a cop's salary meant she had to be a smart shopper. Townsend recognized it because the store was already becoming one of Samyra's favorite places to shop.

"You clean up real nice, Jordan." he said. He looked cool in a linen and silk sport coat in heather green with coordinating slacks and loafers without socks.

"Thanks. You don't look so bad, yourself."

"Hey, what about me?" It didn't matter what Ramsey wore. He looked like he always did--like he just got out of bed—complete with bed hair. His rumpled suit coat covered his .38 revolver. Old school, he was one of the few detectives on the job who eschewed the more modern, higher capacity auto-loaders for what he thought was the more reliable six-shot revolver.

Ignoring his partner, "So where're we going?" Townsend asked.

"A great place for touristas. The Pirates' House. Awesome seafood and great atmosphere in one of Savannah's oldest historic buildings."

"And when you say *historic,* that's a euphemism for haunted, right?" Townsend asked.

"You think I'd take you guys to a haunted restaurant? Moi?" she asked with an evil look on her face and her hand on her chest.

***

Built as a home in 1753, The Pirates' Inn had been used as an inn for visiting seamen since its beginning. Sailors and bloodthirsty pirates had told their stories to each other over libations that had changed with the times for the following nearly three centuries.

Hanging on walls in the Captain's room and the Treasure room were framed pages from rare early editions of Robert Louis Stevenson's iconic work, Treasure Island. In fact Savannah was mentioned several times in the epochal work and it was thought some of the story took place in the Pirates' Inn.

They were led to one of the fifteen dining rooms. Seated at a table for four, eight tables of the same size fitted comfortably in the middle-sized room. After looking over the menu, Lynch and Townsend decided to share a bottle of Hess Collection chardonnay and Ramsey had another Bud Light.

Two cell phones rang simultaneously from diners at different tables. An annoyance one had to put up with from people who felt like they had to stay connected in today's world.

A woman dressed in pirate's garb was giving tours of the restaurant. In the corner of the dining room in which they sat, a Plexiglas-covered, vertical, stone-lined, entrance to a tunnel. According to legend, many an unsuspecting sailor, drinking heavily, would pass out and then be carried through the tunnel to the waterfront and loaded onto a four-masted sailing ship and come to to find himself being spirited away to Shanghai or Singapore, or other locales beyond the continental borders, sometimes taking them years to find their way back. Hence the term "Shanghaied" was introduced into our speech and vernacular.

"Cool place," said Townsend.

"Yeah, good choice," Ramsey agreed.

"Thanks, I love to bring family and friends from out of town, here. It gives them a real taste of the old Savannah."

"Speaking of taste, I'm ready to taste my food." Ramsey was always ready to eat. "Taking down serial killers always makes me hungry." The spicy aroma of Louisiana hot sauce drifted from a nearby table.

"Is that what it is?" Asked Townsend. "I've been wondering."

Almost as if waiting for his cue, a pirate appeared carrying a large tray with their salads. Jordan had a spinach salad and Townsend and Ramsey both had Pirates' House salads.

Noticing her ring finger was unadorned, Ramsey said, "So Jordan, no boyfriend, significant other, anyone important?

"No, you know how it is, a homicide detective, married to the job. Who has time for a relationship, and who's going to put up with it if you did? It'd take a special guy to put up with the hours, bringing the job home and everything else that goes along with it."

"Tell me about it," Ramsey said, "cost me two marriages." He held up two fingers—looked like a peace sign.

"Just one for me," Townsend said, without looking up from his plate, "but who's counting?" He didn't like to talk about it. It was still an open sore.

A different pirate arrived, this time with their dinners. Jordan had the mango chili glazed salmon, Townsend a stuffed flounder and Ramsey, always a big eater, had the seafood harvest platter, basically a sample of everything they had in the kitchen, fried.

"Wow," said Ramsey, "my eyes were bigger than my stomach."

"Not much bigger, partner."

"Now boys," Jordan said, trying to play peacemaker.

"Anyway, bon appetito." Ramsey capitulated.

Returning to talk of the job, "So, do you think we got the right guy for all of the murders?" Lynch asked.

"Are you kidding?" Said Ramsey.

"I've never seen anyone more guilty." Agreed Townsend.

"Wouldn't you like to see inside his head?" Lynch.

"Not me." Said Townsend glibly.

"Me either. I have a feeling his brain is a scary place." Ramsey had dealt with murderers before, but no one as cold-blooded as Wentworth seemed to be.

"Amen to that, partner."

"Enough talking shop. Do you guys have families?" Lynch.

"A daughter, twelve going on thirty-one. Samyra thinks she's the parent and needs to take care of me. In fact I should give her a call, let her know I'll be home tomorrow"

"Not me." Ramsey.

"Me either, unless you count four-legged family. I have a cat—a Maine Coon—Cindy Lauper. She's a sweetheart."

Finishing their dinner, they ordered coffee and desserts. Jordan got key lime pie. Ramsey decided on the banana bread pudding and Townsend a decadent white and dark chocolate mousse.

"I'm going to call Samyra. Be back before the desserts arrive." Townsend stepped out to the lobby to make the call.

"I wish more people would do that—show good manners." Jordan said.

"Yeah I've wanted to shoot people for talking too loud in a restaurant." Ramsey agreed.

Don't do that. I'd have to arrest you." Said Jordan giving the male detective a generous portion of shit.

"Yeah, what makes you think you could catch me?"

"You're joking, right?"

Ignoring the comment, Ramsey said, "By the way, that was a good piece of police work. Getting his picture on the sidewalk, trusting your gut and following through on it. That was some real veteran police work." He tilted his mug of beer in her direction.

"Thanks Nick, I just had a feeling from the first murder."

***

"Yes baby, I'll be home tomorrow, probably around six."

"You got him, daddy?"

'Yeah, we got him."

Yayyy, daddy always gets his man."

Thank you baby. I Love you"

"Love you, daddy. Be careful on the drive back."

"I will. See you tomorrow."

***

"How's Samyra?" Ramsey

"She's fine. She sends her love."

"Thanks."

"Yeah, and she thinks it's cool that a female detective caught a serial killer. She wants to be a homicide detective.

"Maybe I could talk to her sometime. Give her some guidance."

"If she continues with that idea, yeah, that'd be nice. I'd appreciate it." *Hope she doesn't though.*

The coffee and desserts arrived causing a pause in the talking. Ramsey said, "That woman over there looks like my second wife." He shuddered. *Glad I've finished eating. Wouldn't want to lose my dinner.*

"That key lime pie was delicious," Jordan said.

"So was the bread pudding," said Ramsey.

"Well, I think I won with the white and dark chocolate mousse." Townsend.

"Yeah, the golden boy always wins," said Ramsey.

Jordan pulled out a gold American Express card and said, "Well, this one's on the city of Savannah tonight."

"Hey, all right. I would have had another beer if I'd known that," said Ramsey.

"And I'd've picked out an even better wine," Townsend said.

After paying the tab, Jordan said, "You want to call it a night?"

'Probably should," said Townsend. "Gonna have a busy day tomorrow, getting our boy home.

"Yep, we got to take care of our cargo." Ramsey.

Jordan dropped off Anthony and Nick at their hotel and made her way to her townhouse a few blocks south of the city center. It looked like a historic home but it was a new construction built to look that way. Pulling up out front, she could see her upstairs bedroom curtain move, but nothing to be alarmed by, it was just Cindy Lauper.

Chapter 15
Going Home

The truck arrived at 11:30 a.m. Lynch's boss signed the paperwork brought by the officers from APD making the handoff legal. He turned over a fairly substantial amount of cash Wentworth had had on him, a cheap watch and a plastic trashbag containing the clothes he wore. He was now officially their responsibility. Townsend and Ramsey updated the two uniformed officers about all that had happened and it was decided that the detectives would follow the transport truck giving them four men responsible for taking care of him on the roughly three-and-three-quarter hour trip to Atlanta.

Escorted to the truck shackled in handcuffs and leg irons, Wentworth seemed to think this would all work out.

"Good morning officers, detectives," he greeted them. Still trying to make them doubt themselves, wonder if they'd made a mistake, gotten the wrong guy. "Let's get this settled, move on, so I can get on with my life and you gentlemen can start chasing real criminals." Listening to him, Detective Townsend looked at Ramsey and just shook his head. "He's good," said Ramsey.

"Real good," said Townsend.

"Enough talking," said Ramsey, lifting Wentworth into the back of the truck by his the waistband of his pants, "Let's get rolling." Townsend and Ramsey would follow the truck closely, keeping an eye on it, just on the chance that something might happen.

The plan was not to make any stops. Both vehicles had been filled up and the cops had water for themselves and Wentworth.

Everything went as planned until the uniformed cops radioed Townsend and Ramsey.

"Wentworth needs to take a leak." Banging on the truck's wall to get their attention he'd made his needs apparent.

"Fuck him. I'm older than him and I can make it. Tell him to hold it. He needs a prostate exam. Course he'll get a lot of those in prison," Ramsey chuckled at the uncomfortable humor. He was pissed, not wanting to deviate from the plan.

"You know I can't do that, detective. We have to give him every consideration or human rights groups will be up in arms saying we've violated his rights. There's a truckstop at the next exit. Let's just stop, get it done real quick-like and get back on the road. Depending on the trafffic, we've only got another thirty or forty-five minutes."

"All right, goddammit."

He told Townsend, "You got the gist of it. He needs to take a piss. We can't violate his goddamn human rights. What about his victims' rights to life? We'll stop at the next fucking exit, a truckstop."

Once they passed the sign indicating they were a mile from the exit the detectives passed the truck to get there first. Pulled up in front of the Valero Truckstop, where Townsend parked in the fire zone. The detectives exited the patrol car and weapons drawn, waited as the transport pulled in right behind their car. The uniforms climbed out of the cab and pulled their weapons, and with Townsend and Ramsey covering them, they opened the rear door and helped out the accused serial killer.

Wentworth got out of the dark transport, squinting from the bright sunlight and moving slowly from stiffness; still cuffed and shackled he wasn't going anywhere very fast. He looked directly up at the bright sun making himself sneeze. "What, no God bless you?" They all ignored him.

The uniforms flanking him and the detectives behind, they escorted him to the mens' restroom.

Passing two pre-teenage boys, staring at him in his chains, he raised his cuffed hands in the universal imaginary gun position and shot them. Then gave them a quick wink.

The uniforms walked him in and one said, "Urinal."

"No privacy?"

"You better get used to it where you're going."

The detectives were drinking coffee when they returned.

Wentworth said, "How about a Mountain Dew?"

"You got any money?" said Ramsey. "Oh yeah, no you don't. That's because you're going to jail. Sorry. Besides you'd probably just have to piss again.

Chapter 16
The Case

Wentworth was booked into the City of Atlanta Detention Center. A massive six story concrete monolith, it was as large as some state prisons. Located on the south end of Peachtree Street, for the prisoners it housed it was psychologically much further away from the bars, restaurants and nightlife on the Buckhead end of Peachtree.

The police reports for the murders in Atlanta had been forwarded to the Fulton County DA. It was his decision to make whether or not to bring charges against Wentworth or to send it to a Grand Jury to be decided. In such a high profile case as this one, the DA sent it to the Grand Jury due to it meeting in secret without the prisoner or his attorney present and him not having to present all the evidence in an open forum for the defense attorney to know what the state had.

***

In the harsh light of a jail cell, Bad Penny's bad attitude returned.

"Hey asshole," he said to one of the guards, "when do I get some god damn food?"

"You'll eat when we say you eat," came the curt reply from somewhere else in the jail.

"Yeah, well fuck you."

"Fuck you. I'm going home tonight for supper and a beer and you'll still be in jail."

Wentworth was assigned a public defender, Benjamin Wasserman. He was a graduate of Atlanta's Emory University School of Law. One of the top twenty law schools in the country, it was unusual for any of its graduates to work as a public defender, but young Ben felt an obligation, borne out of his father's humble beginnings, and realizing that he was a damn good attorney, to work for those who couldn't afford a high profile attorney the cost of whom could eat up a family's savings. He wasn't much older than Bad Penny and with his pompadour-like haircut he looked like either a television evangelist or an ambulance chaser who advertised on television, of which he was neither. After breakfast the following morning they met for the first time.

Meeting in a small room setup for that purpose, they tap danced around each other.

"I'm Ben Wasserman, assigned to represent you."

"Bad Penny."

"Your name is Pennington Wentworth II and that's what you'll call yourself from now on."

"I don't know what you're talking about. That's what those cops called me but I don't remember anything about that name.

"So you're saying you have amnesia?"

"No, no. I don't know. Maybe. I guess. Hell yeah I do." He was smart enough to figure out that if he had amnesia it could aid in his defense.

Have you had an injury, illness, anything that could have caused memory loss?

"I don't remember," he said laughing and slapping his knee.

"Mr. Wentworth, I assure you, what you're accused of is no laughing matter."

"Sorry. Yeah, my head hurts all the time and I have this scar under my hairline, but I don't know what caused it." Pennington lifted the hair on the front of his head revealing a three-inch long scar, indicating a recent surgery.

"I see. That's enlightening. It won't be hard to discover what happened there. I have two investigators that work for our office. I'll get them right on it." The Grand Jury will meet early next week to determine what charges will be brought against you. I'll see you after I hear from them." Wasserman stood up to leave and shook hands with Pennington.

A massive African-American officer whose shirt sleeves were bursting at the seams from trying to cover his cantaloupe-size biceps came for Wentworth and returned him to his cell. He responded to the catcalls, whistles and shouted threats from other prisoners on the block with glares, clenched fists and threats of his own.

The cell door was opened and Bad Penny said, "Thanks for nothing, dumbass."

Through the bars the large gentleman said, "Let me give you a bit of friendly advice. Try to get along. As long as you're here or where ever you go after this, life will be better if you try to fit in. Believe me, there are some men in here who will fuck you up. Give you a beating like you couldn't imagine in your worst nightmare. That's after they make you their bitch. Won't kill you, though. This will be worse. Make you wish you were dead. Be in a hospital bed, eating through a tube in your stomach, somebody changing your diaper, for the rest of your life."

"Aiiight."

"Trust me on this, son. I don't care how many people you killed. You ain't as bad as you think you are." The large man could tell his sage advice wouldn't be heeded.

***

Gerry Lovett had worked as an investigator for over three years. She applied for a secretarial position, was hired, and after a year was transferred to investigations. Being a woman, she thought it gave her empathy that aided her in doing her job and she also thought it disarmed the interviewees, set them at ease and caused them to trust her and to help her get the information she needed. She went to law school at night, was going to be an attorney, but she wanted to be a prosecutor. She saw too many scumbags get off. Didn't like it.

The first thing she did was use the best friend of anyone seeking information. She performed a Google search on Pennington Wentworth, II. Found out he was quite wealthy due to an inheritance from his deceased parents. No other family. Graduated college but never held what one would call a real job. Never married. His Facebook page was helpful. Group pictures of him with men and women, usually holding a glass of white wine or a cosmopolitan. He had friends but no apparent serious girlfriends.

Then she started contacting hospitals, found out he'd been in an accident, suffered a traumatic brain injury. One day investigating and she had a great deal of information for Ben. Hopefully enough to help him successfully defend his client. She wanted Ben to be successful even if she thought the clients weren't always innocent.

She could hear Ben on the phone when she knocked on his closed door.

"Enter."

She did as she was told and he gestured to one of the two chairs fronting his large mahogany desk. He said into the phone, "Look, I've got a meeting. Let's talk about this later. Yeah, over racquetball."

He cradled the phone. "Whatcha got?"

"Whatcha want?"

"Everything, good and bad."

"He was born with a silver spoon in his mouth. Has millions from an inheritance. Deceased parents. They died in a car accident when he was in college. Got called out of class on a Tuesday morning only to be told both his parents were dead. I think it's admirable that he completed his degree requirements, considering he inherited mid-eight figures. Of course, it *was* a degree in literature. No other family. Might be gay. Not that there's anything wrong with that." She loved that line from the old Seinfeld episode. "If he's not, he missed a good chance to be. There's no evidence that he has or has had a serious girlfriend."

"He was in that huge pile up on 400 a few weeks back. That's when he got the head injury. Spent two weeks in Grady. At the time, they were concerned about personality change caused by a TBI. In fact they sent him home with a friend, female; he wasn't supposed to be alone. From the way he was before I'm guessing that's what flipped a switch in his brain. There's nothing in his past to indicate he'd commit these types of crimes. Only blip seemed to be a tendency to speed."

"Millions, huh? Find the friend. Talk to her. Find out what she knows."

She went back to his Facebook page. Looked like his closest friend was Ashley Denson. Found her phone number online. It made her wonder if anyone used phonebooks anymore, or landlines. She doubted it. But she was curious now and she'd find out. Curiosity was the best trait for an investigator.

She called Miss Denson and explained that she was an investigator working for the attorney defending Wentworth and she wondered if she had time to meet to help her friend.

Miss Denson said she'd be happy to meet Lovett at the local Starbucks near her Buckhead location real estate office. She had, it seemed, according to her, an unnatural desire for skinny cinnamon dolce lattes. Her local Starbucks was in a Barnes and Noble on Peachtree Street about a block and a half south of the Peachtree St.-Roswell Rd. split, ground zero for Buckhead and all its accompanying nightlife.

Ashley entered and went straight to the counter, a woman on a mission, and got her usual grande' skinny cinnamon dolce latte.

Looked around and seeing only one woman sitting alone assumed it was the investigator. Lovett had chosen a table in front of a huge window that overlooked Peachtree Street, the broad avenue that was the main artery of commerce and entertainment in Atlanta. Hundreds of cars passing by every hour.

Lovett recognized her instantly from the pictures on Wentworth's Facebook page. She removed all doubt for Miss Denson by smiling and standing to greet her. "Thank you for agreeing to meet with me, Miss Denson."

"My pleasure, but please, call me Ashley. And thank you for letting me pick the place. In addition to being a Starbucks snob I'm also a voracious reader so I love coming here."

"I'm a big reader, too. Who're your favorite authors?"

I have many favorites—John Grisham, Lincoln Child, C.J. Box— really there are too many to name them all. What about you?

"Well, Being in the justice system, I love Linda Fairstein, among, like you, many others."

"Oh, me too. I forgot about her."

"Before I get sidetracked talking about books, so, what can you tell me about Wentworth, er, Pennington?"

"I was just stunned to hear of his arrest. I still can't get over it. The Pennington I've known for so long—well, it's just unthinkable. He's always been the sweetest guy you'd ever want to meet. Quiet, gentle, a pacifist, really; a little effeminate, respectful. Open to diversity, a vegetarian, just a gentle soul; would rather someone hurt him than to hurt somebody. He certainly wasn't profligate. At the very worst he's a bit of a scamp. He's always liked to play tricks on friends."

"I understand you picked him up from the hospital after his stay."

"Yes, that's when I first noticed the change. I guess that's when it started."

"How so?"

"Well, I'm sure you know, or will find out anyway. He had a fractured skull in a car accident. He was in intensive care and a regular hospital room for a total of two weeks. He called me to ask if I'd pick him up. Actually, if I recall correctly, he *told* me to come pick him up and got angry when I couldn't get there sooner, and he was so profane. I'd never heard him use swear words before that day. He just seemed so angry and impatient and he'd never been that way before—just so very patient and kind." She paused. "If I may ask, what do you all think you can do to help him?"

" I'm not privy to exactly what Ben's thinking, that's Ben Wasserman, my boss, the lawyer working for Pennington. He's a wonderful attorney, and a deeply caring man, and I suspect he'll want to pursue the line that he has mental problems due to his head injury.

"Well, I hope Mr. Wasserman can help him. I mean if he did what they said he did, the Pennington I know, I mean knew, *before*—his injury—could never have killed those people.

"Well, we'll see. Thank you for the information and your help."

"You're very welcome. Good luck. Let me know if I can help you with anything else."

"Thanks. Will do."

***

It was almost noon when Lovett got to the office. Ben was on his way out for a lunch meeting.

They stopped on the sidewalk and he asked, "Anything good?"

"Yeah, boss, she gave me a good picture of him."

"I have a lunch meeting. Hold it til I get back."

"No problem. It'll wait."

***

Wasserman knocked on Lovett's door. "You ready?"

"Be right there."

His walls were papered with his college diploma from the University of Georgia, his law school diploma from Emory, and other awards and proclamations. Lovett sat in front of his desk. She hoped she'd have her law degree before too long. Another year going to school at night should do it.

"So whatta you got?"

'If she's being honest, and I have no reason to doubt her veracity, he was the meekest, mildest, milquetoast, little lamb you've ever known before the crash. Sounds like he suffered a traumatic brain injury, a TBI in medical jargon, in the crash—changed everything about him."

"Good, sounds like that's our play. Now we have to wait and see what the Grand Jury comes back with."

***

The biggest thing Bad Penny had to get used to were the sounds of the night. The sounds of inmates farting, sobbing, moaning—from jerking off, but the worst was when they fell asleep and with it came the deafening roar from the sound of silence.

The detention center had the same smell as bigger prisons. The smell of shit, piss and semen. Masturbation was as common to prisoners as eating or drinking was to those un-incarcerated.

Bad Penny got tired of the moaning and yelled out in the dark, "Hey, you goddamn perverts—you're gonna go blind!"

His first Monday in the detention center was no different than any other day. That was both good and bad. It had been medically proven that more heart attacks and strokes occur on Mondays due to the stress of starting the work week. He didn't have to worry about that, which was good, but he was unable to look forward to the weekend, which wasn't. At seven a.m. they were taken to the cafeteria for breakfast. The food wasn't healthy, but it was filling. Sausage, potatoes, eggs and all the coffee one could drink. All the major food groups. Protein, carbs and fats. And caffeine. The only difference in breakfast and other meals was no eggs at the others.

Bad Penny stayed to himself. He wasn't scared, mostly annoyed and just basically pissed off with the way everybody else acted. Losers or they wouldn't be there. The blacks stayed with the blacks, except for the ones that were muslim—they had their own group, same with the whites and the Mexicans didn't like anybody, including each other. Everybody tried to look badder than everybody else. He tried to stay by himself at meals. It was the only time he had to be around anyone else and he'd tough it out.

***

The Grand Jury met on Tuesday morning. Ben would contact the district attorney to get the results that afternoon.

He had a busy morning tying up loose ends on his previous case. A manslaughter charge against his client for killing someone while driving under the influence. A sad situation: he was a successful high-tech salesman from out of town, entertaining a client at dinner, got behind the wheel of his Mercedes after having at least one too many martinis, and killed a young mother. He didn't stand a chance when the handsome young husband, sitting with his toddler on his lap, testified how he and his young daughter's lives were ruined.

"Jonathan, Ben Wasserman, attorney for Pennington Wentworth, here." Ben respected and even liked Jonathan Drake. He'd defended clients before him only twice before since he usually went up against one of his assistant prosecutors. Drake had a reputation of being tough, but fair, and personable, some would say charismatic, and he'd done nothing to disprove that reputation when Ben faced off against him. Speculation was he'd run for state-wide office when he tired of being a prosecutor and some thought that a run at the U.S. House of Representatives or even a run at a U.S. Senate seat was in his future.

"Yeah Ben, I guess you want to know the charges against your client."

"You read my mind."

"You're easy to read, Ben. And, this won't be a surprise to you, I'm sure. One count of second degree murder, six counts of murder in the first."

"Damn."

"Yeah, they're giving him a break on the first one. Going for the gold on all the rest. I can email you the paperwork."

"Okay, thanks Jon."

"Welcome. See you between the hedges." Drake graduated from UGA and that was him paying homage to the football team, the Bulldogs, due to their Athens, GA stadium having tall hedges lining both sides of the field.

***

Ben walked from his downtown office to the Detention Center early Wednesday morning to meet with Wentworth and update him about the charges and his plans for a defense strategy.

***

A different huge African-American guard approached Bad Penny's cell. "Wentworth."

"Yeah, what is it?"

"You got a visitor."

"Who is it? I hope it's the goddamn governor, coming to pay his respects."

"Your lawyer, and you better be nice to him. He's trying to keep your sorry ass alive."

"He better be nice to *me*. I'm going to make his goddamn bones. Win or lose, his name is going to be on the fucking television every goddamn night because of me."

"Yeah, you're a big shot, aren't you?"

"You're damn right I'm a big shot. I would've been the all-time record breaking serial killer in the U.S. of fucking A., if they hadn't gotten lucky."

"Sure you would've. Just step back so I can open the door."

Ben was waiting in the sterile, institutional green, vinyl and tiled interview room when Wentworth was escorted in. He wondered if the same guy sold the same tiled floor and vinyl chairs and sofas to every jail in every city. They all looked the same.

Pennington entered. He looked even smaller than he actually was next to the massive officer escorting him.

Ben said, "Thank you officer." Then, "Good to see you Pennington. How're you holding up?"

"You too, Ben." Bad Penny called him by his first name on purpose, to level the playing field and to let him know that they were equals. That his attorney was no better than him.

"I'm holding up okay. I could use some better food though. I need some fucking steaks and some hamburgers. I need to keep my protein intake up so I can keep building muscle."

"Well, I don't think I can help you there, Pennington. But I need to tell you what the Grand Jury brought back."

"The first one, John Matthew, second degree. The other six, first degree. My investigator talked to Grady Hospital and friends of yours and it appears that you had a TBI, a traumatic brain injury, in a car accident. A massive multi-car pileup. Caused personality change, aggression, amnesia, and other issues. That will probably be our defense."

He pulled out a file folder. "I want you to look this over and I'll come back the day after tomorrow and you can give me your thoughts, what you remember and anything else that stands out to you.

"Aiiight."

Opening his wallet, Ben said, 'here's my card— have a guard call me if you need me."

"Thanks. But I'm good."

***

After stopping by an Apple Store to check out the latest and greatest iPad, Wasserman returned to his office. Was having an open-faced Reuben at his desk, and not just because he was Jewish. He liked the lean pastrami piled high and heavy on the Thousand Island dressing.

"Did you see him?" Lovett asked.

"Yeah. I saw him."

"So what's going on?"

"I don't know. He's either a hardass or a dumbass. I haven't figured out which, yet. He just doesn't get it that I'm trying to save his life. And believe me they will stick a needle in his dumb ass and kill him, unless I'm as good as I think I am.

"Well, we know you're as good as you think you are. But lets hope he comes around because you'll need his cooperation to save his sorry ass.

"Yeah, let's hope."

***

Bad Penny had stayed in the concrete hell of his cell except for going to meals and meeting his lawyer for almost a week, so he decided he would go outside today in the allotted time to get some fresh air and to see if he could get some exercise. A large open area adjacent to the rear of the building, there were no weights or anything an inmate could use as a weapon, so he would use the only thing he had, his own body. He did all manner of pushups. Normal, narrow grip, wide grip, clapping pushups, T-pushups, elevated, and using the curb on a sidewalk; inclined and declined. He then moved to lower body and did narrow stance bodyweight squats, wide stance, sumo squats, regular lunges, twisting lunges and prisoner lunges. He thought that last term was especially appropriate.

In less than an hour he'd gotten what he felt was a better workout than one with barbells. He knew what he would do everyday now and he didn't even have to go outside to do them. He could do it all in his cell.

After his workout Penny went to the shower area. A large room with shower heads on all four walls. It was empty but for him. Wasn't long however before one of the Mexicans he'd seen in the yard entered. The large man rippled with brown muscle, the result of most of a lifetime spent in prison gyms. He got too close for comfort for such a large room.

"I saw you work out, meng. You think you're a hard ass, no? I think I want to find out how hard that ass is."

He put both hands on Bad Penny's shoulders and with abnormal strength, forced Penny to his knees, in front of him. "And you better do it good, meng," he said.

Bad Penny took a deep breath, and with no other choice...and with fingers laced together hit him as hard as he could with both fists, in the groin, then grabbing him by the balls and twisting them in his clenched fists, pulled him to the floor and head-butted the big latino in the face, shattering all of his upper and lower front teeth.

To the unconscious form lying in the spray of the shower, he said, "So, was it hard enough for you, asshole?"

When he went to supper, word had obviously gotten around about his encounter with the large latino dude. All of the Mexicans just glared. No idea what that meant, respect or fear or intimidation. So, he glared back. It might have been respect, or it could've been a look of, *just wait, you'll get yours.* He had no idea how this thing would play out.

***

Ben Wasserman took his calling seriously. He felt strongly about providing his clients the best defense of which he was capable, no matter how he felt about them personally or about what they were accused of. On that, he never wavered.

He entered the interview room that he was growing accustomed to. The same behemoth as the last time escorted Wentworth. He was glad someone that size was on the side of the good guys. Ben knew they'd be there awhile. He needed something to help him get through it. He went over to the cheap coffee maker sitting on a folding card table in the corner and poured himself a cup. It smelled burnt. He added powdered creamer and two splendas. "You want a cup, Pennington?"

"Aiiight."

"How do you want it?"

"Black. The way real men drink their coffee." Ben didn't think he meant it as a dig toward him, that it was directed inwardly instead.

"So, did you look at the paperwork? Any thoughts?"

"Nah, man, I've been busy."

The stunned look on Mr. Wasserman's face showed incredulity.

Bad Penny, laughed out loud. "I'm just busting your balls. Yeah, I looked at it."

"So what do you think? Let's take them in order. Matthew:"

"That was the asshole?"

"Why do you call him that?"

"That's what I called him before I caved in his skull with a two by four."

"Why?"

"Why what?"

"Why did you call him that?"

"Because he was one."

Mr. Wasserman sighed deeply.

"I don't remember why I did it. I just know he was an asshole."

"So you killed him."

"He deserved it."

"Okaaay, moving on. Cinnamon, real name, Kathryn Smith. Tell me about that one."

"What about it?"

"What happened? And Pennington, if we're going to do this I need you to cooperate. Stop being obtuse."

"Well, we met at the club where she danced, she invited me back to her place, and long story short, she tried to make me pay for pussy."

"So you killed her."

"So I killed her. She deserved it."

"She deserved it too? I'm beginning to see a pattern here."

"It is what it is."

"Number three, Spalding."

"He really deserved it."

"Why?"

"He was an effeminate bastard and for some reason I just hate effeminate guys. I don't know why. But I have the feeling he'd done something to me."

"This ought to be a good one. Number four, the priest, Monsignor

Francis O'Brien, tell me about this one. I can't wait."

"Simple, I just worried that he'd tell someone about my confession."

"Number five: Sheryl Watson."

"She was stupid—leaving a bar with a stranger she'd just met."

"So you killed her because she was stupid?"

'Somebody had to."

Number six: The barber, Mr. Robert Bowden. Tell me about him. Kind of out of your norm."

"Easy. He wouldn't shut up. He just annoyed the shit out of me. Wanted me to look at pictures of his goddamn grandchildren. I mean "Please". Do I look like the type who would want to see pictures of his grandchildren? I couldn't care less.

"Lucky number seven, Miss Tess Chu."

'Easy again. I'd killed only whites, albeit, women, men and girly-boys. I needed to kill an Asian, to show I was an equal opportunity killer.

"Okay Pennington. It's only about three weeks until the trial. So we'll need to meet more often. The District Attorney wants to fast track it. There's a lot of public interest in it."

"Aiiight. You know where to find me. Just remember, I'm your meal ticket."

Ben buzzed for a guard and as his client was escorted out, just shook his head at Pennington's apparent lack of interest.

***

"So how's it going?" Lovett asked.

"I've never seen anything like it. That head injury turned him into a complete psychopath. He has a complete and total callous disregard for other people. He has no empathy whatsoever. Killing people because they annoyed him, talked too much. He thought they were stupid. Because one was Asian. Killed the stripper because she wanted to charge him for sex. I mean, sheesh. Anything could set him off."

"What do you need me to do?"

"Talk to his friends. Start with Miss Denson. Find out from her who his other friends are. Doctors, teachers, ministers, anyone else you can think of. Oh, and see if you can talk to the neurosurgeon who worked on him. If nothing else works I'll need to baffle them with bullshit, the medical kind. We're going to have to line everyone up to testify. Create a clear distinction between how he was before the accident and how he is now.

"You got it, boss."

***

After meeting with Miss Denson again, Lovett spent the next week talking to everyone that Ben had suggested, up to and including his favorite barista at Starbucks and his fifth grade teacher. He drank cinnamon dolce lattes with extra cinnamon before. Ben knew for a fact he drank his coffee black with no flavor or sweeteners now. Even that small detail was probably significant.

The friends consisted of two effeminate men in their thirties and two other pretty women, also in their thirties who like Miss Denson, were all willing to testify about his pacifism, his quietness, sweetness and lack of aggression or even a bad temper. The neurosurgeon compared his case to one in the 1800s when one Phineas Gage had a large iron rod driven completely through his head by an explosion, destroying most of his left frontal lobe. A famous case studied by neurologists, psychologists and other medical professionals, much was written about the subject's personality change, and complete turnaround from his previous life, in texts and curricula of various disciplines.

***

Bad Penny worked out every day, both outside and in his cell. He was now doing one thousand pushups a day along with a thousand bodyweight squats. His upper body and legs were packing on rippling muscle and he looked more intimidating by the moment, something that he thought would help him survive in the detention center or any prison in which he might end up.

He was beginning to resign himself to the probability that he might never be free.

On Fridays a book cart made its rounds of the cells. He picked out books on law, exercise and history, the last one only because he had an idle curiosity about the world since he could remember almost nothing of what he might have learned in school.

Although Bad Penny had guessed he didn't have any family or

friends, or at least not many, the fact that he'd had no visitors except for his attorney, he felt that that, confirmed it.

***

Bad Penny was growing accustomed to the smell of shit and piss and he was becoming oblivious to seeing inmates masturbating. In the showers, in their cells as he passed by, in obscure corners, wherever they might find themselves.

With the new week's arrival, he volunteered to work on a cleanup crew just to give himself extra time out of the cell. A couple of hours three days a week was the voluntary commitment. Different groups of prisoners worked on each floor and the crew was the same unless someone had served their time and was released, and like him, someone new was added. There were a dozen inmates on the third floor crew on which he worked. A mix of caucasians, Mexicans and blacks.

Second day on the crew Bad Penny was sent to a large utility storeroom to get supplies. He unlocked the door and left it unlocked until he would exit. A moment later the click of the doorknob turning. From over his shoulder he heard, "You should've locked the door, meng."

Three of the Mexicans on the crew were blocking the closed door.

"You fucked up our friend, meng. Now it's your turn to get fucked up."

"Aiiight. Give it your best, you fucking taco jockey."

The three separated and advanced on him. Bad Penny held a steel-handled mop. Picking up a metal pail on rollers, he slung it at the first one's head, causing him to duck and distracting him long enough for Bad Penny to take a grand slam swing at his head with the heavy-handled mop. Connecting with a force powered by adrenalin and his large amounts of new muscle, the big man dropped; his brain stopped functioning before he hit the storeroom floor.

With a direct thrust to his solar plexus, he impaled number two in the body with the long metal handle, killing him immediately, as a torrent of hot, coppery-smelling blood erupted from his mouth.

Number three decided that his friends weren't worth dying for and left without looking directly at Bad Penny.

He shouted at his back, "Smart fucking decision."

Returning to the cleanup crew, he told them, "We should probably clean the storeroom today." He led them to the two bodies and while they cleaned up the mess, he found the guard that was supposed to be in charge of them and told him what'd happened. The man would lose his job over the incident.

Bad Penny knew it was self defense and he had nothing to worry about except revenge. And so far, that was proving only to be annoying rather than particularly worrisome.

***

After breakfast the next morning, a guard stopped him on his way back to his cell and said "Interview room. Your attorney."

He entered, saw Mr. Wasserman, and said, "Barrister, this is a pleasant surprise."

Ben shook his hand and said, "Not so pleasant Pennington, I'm afraid."

"What's up?"

"I heard about the incident."

"What? What incident? There's been an incident?" Then a pause, "Had you goin' there for a second, didn't I counselor?"

"Pennington, you've got to get serious about this. Your life is at stake."

"Ben, you just haven't figured it out yet. I don't give a flying fuck."

"Well, I'm glad one of us cares."

"All I care about now is making us famous."

Looking at his notes, Ben said, "Anyway, I need to let you know where we stand. I plan on using your head injury as a defense; it changed you to your very core. My assistant, Ms. Lovett has run down friends, acquaintances, people you know, and all are willing to testify as to what kind of person you were before the change. That part is easy. The second part is harder. As long I can show you didn't know right from wrong I'm confident I can have you confined to a mental hospital, an institution."

"Hold on, now, Ben, hold on. I don't know if I can go along with that. I don't think I could live in a loony bin."

"At least you'd be alive."

"What are you saying, Ben?"

"The great state of Georgia has the death penalty, Pennington. But the good news is those two inmates you killed, they can't use those against you. It's pretty obvious those were self defense. But don't forget, when the trial is over here you'll have to go back to Savannah to face those charges."

"Well fuck. What method of execution do they use in this state anyway?"

"The same as in thirty-four other states, Pennington, lethal injection. And from what I understand it isn't pleasant." Ben rose and shook his clients hand. "I'll be back soon. Mostly to start reviewing courtroom procedure with you. You need to know how to act in court…and dress. Do you have a suit?"

"I don't know if it made it here or not."

"Don't worry about it. I'll get you one. What size do you wear?"

"I don't know. Been working out, putting on muscle. I'm getting huge."

"You look like about a 42-reg to me. We'll try that."

"I can't wait."

They shook hands again and after Ben pushed the button sounding a buzzer that they were done, the guard came for Bad Penny.

***

Bad Penny's reputation was growing. As he was escorted back to his cell there were no catcalls or sounds of derision, even from the Mexicans. And the white inmates started a slow, respectful clap for him. He puffed out his chest even further. *Hell yeah, I'm a fucking bad ass.*

Getting back in his cell, he decided to take a nap. During his research into muscle building he learned that it wasn't really lifting weights or body weight exercise that builds muscle; it grows during the rest and sleep you get after the workout. Working out tears down the muscle and one grows new muscle and bigger muscle while one sleeps. That's why so many prison inmates looked like professional bodybuilders, because all they do is eat, workout and sleep. It was the perfect formula for making them huge.

***

The inmates were supposed to be taken to lunch at noon. At 12:03 it hadn't happened. Bad Penny shouted at the top of his lungs. "When are we going to get some goddamn lunch?" That started all the inmates yelling.

Two minutes later their doors opened and to the guards nearest him, he said, "Fucking retards. Can't even get us to our goddamn lunch on time."

In the cafeteria line he saw the food and to the serving inmates, said, "Shit, fish again? It's not even Friday. I'm a fucking Catholic and I don't even want fish on Friday. I sure as fuck don't want it on other days. How about some goddamn beef?"

After lunch the clean up crews assembled to do their work. Bad Penny was the unofficial leader of his crew, now. Killing two other members and causing a third to quit would cause that to happen.

***

On Monday morning Mr. Wasserman came in. "Well Pennington, the trial starts Wednesday. I'm ready. I hope you are."

"As long as you are, Counselor, we'll be fine," Bad Penny said.

"Yeah, well I hope we're on the same page. I've left you a suit, shirt, tie and shoes in the office." I guessed you at a size nine shoe."

"Good guess, Counselor."

"I'll see you Wednesday. Uniformed police officers will deliver you to the courthouse. I'll see you there."

Chapter 17
The First Trial

It was a short five minute walk from the detention center to the Fulton County Courthouse, but the officers drove him in a marked patrol car for his own protection. The APD had received threats against Wentworth and although it might not be there first choice of duty, they took their assignment of protecting him, and the threats, seriously.

Ben was there early, sitting in his chair at the defense's table. Wentworth's escorts brought him over then positioned themselves near the entrances to the large room.

"Good morning, Counselor."

"Good morning, Pennington."

"How ya doin?"

"Fine. Thank you. I hope you're as well as can be as expected."

"I'm okay. I hope you're ready to give them a show. If you do this right, Ben, you'll be set for life. Getting one of the most prolific serial killers of all time off."

"Well Pennington, in my judgement you're a sick man and belong in an institution, not in prison. Just remember, you're not going to testify and the jury can't hold that against you. But while you're at this table, no smirks, screwed up faces, gestures, fidgeting, or sounds. I don't care what anyone says about you. I don't want to see a reaction, because if I see it, the jury will see it and you'll be done."

"Aiiight."

"Poker face, Pennington."

"I said aiiight, dammit."

"That's what I'm talking about. If I can do it to you, the prosecutor can. He's good, the best. The DA himself is trying you."

"Good, the best should try the worst."

People began arriving and filling the room. Among them, the District Attorney, Jonathan Drake, with his platoon of assistants, arrived.

"Good morning, Ben."

"Good morning, Sir." Ben chose to address the District Attorney respectfully inside the walls of the courtroom. Hopefully, it couldn't hurt to try and butter him up, either. He might need a job someday. The DA wore a navy blue suit with a red tie looped around the collar of a startlingly white dress shirt. In stark contrast to Ben's own sober gray, chalk pinstripe suit with a muted purple necktie.

At five minutes until nine, the bailiff brought in a tray with a pitcher of water, a glass and a bowl of peppermints for the judge and placed them near his gavel. He took his place standing at attention to be near the judge's side. At precisely nine o'clock, he spoke:

"All rise. Hear ye, hear ye. The District Court for the City of Atlanta is now in session, the honorable Judge William Stephens presiding." The judge entered from his chambers. Judge Stephens was known to run a tight ship, his courtroom not a place in which you wanted to screw up. It would mess up one's day if one were to incur his wrath.

"Are all present?" he asked.

"Jonathan Drake present for the state, your honor."

"Benjamin Wasserman present for the defense, your honor."

"Is the state ready to present its case?'

"We are, your honor."

"Please proceed."

In criminal cases, the prosecutor, orchestrates the trial, sets the pace and makes the decisions as to how the trial will be conducted, with the judge overseeing it to make sure it is done according to law and procedure. The district attorney would make his opening statement and could either outline the charges against the defendant in a short statement or begin to make his case, in a longer statement, at his discretion.

"Your honor and members of the jury, the state will show that the defendant, Pennington Wentworth, II, did, with malice and forethought, cause the deaths of seven people. The evidence presented will prove beyond a reasonable doubt that the defendant did in fact, commit the crimes with which he is accused. In six of the deaths the charges are 1st degree murder and in the seventh, the charge is 2nd degree murder. The state will ask the members of the jury to return a verdict of guilty on each individual charge with no option for lesser charges.

Ben thought it telling that the DA didn't give the jury the option of returning verdicts of lesser charges. That meant that he was convinced of the strength of his case. He expected a guilty verdict on each individual count.

The first witnesses Mr. Drake called were two people, including the Sage manager, who testified that the defendant was the person who argued with John Matthew, less than thirty minutes before the young man was hit by a piece of two by four, causing a skull fracture from which he died the following day. There was no physical evidence presented, but on cross examination the witnesses held that the defendant was the person they saw arguing with Mr. Matthew minutes before he was assaulted and had left Sage shortly before the victim.

For victim number two, Kathryn Smith, aka Cinnamon, the stripper, witnesses, other employees of the club testified that Pennington Wentworth talked with the victim, paid her for dances and ultimately left with her.

The most damning evidence was the DNA trace from the semen he deposited in her vagina and mouth. Ben tried to create doubt by suggesting that Pennington left with her, and had sex with her but that didn't mean that he killed her. An example of a defense attorney throwing something against the wall and hoping it would stick. The looks on the members of the jury's faces showed they weren't buying it.

That testimony took most of the morning so the judge called a recess to break for lunch. Ben sent his young assistant, Michael Jones to a food truck on the street outside from which he'd picked up a menu on his way into court, to get sandwiches for the defense team and their client. Ben ordered a turkey Reuben, Michael got a cheeseburger, Gerry chose a Cobb salad and Wentworth ordered a half pound bacon cheeseburger with extra cheese, ketchup, mustard and onion. Michael returned with the food and after they moved to a small conference room to eat, one of the uniformed policemen escorted Wentworth along side the others, then positioned himself on the other side of the one door into the small room. Michael passed out the food and Bad Penny unwrapped the paper from his burger and took a large bite. The look on his face showed his displeasure. He raised up half way and tossed the burger into a small trash can in the corner and said, "They put mayonnaise on my fucking burger. They better be glad I wasn't there to see it happen or they'd regret it."

For the first time Ben and his team had seen an example of Pennington's explosive temper going off at the smallest slight, a minor annoyance, a mild irritant. An example of his complete and utter lack of empathy, his inability to function in everyday life.

Returning from lunch, the DA started the afternoon session with the charge of murder of Mark Spalding, the weakest link in their case for multiple murders. No one had seen the victim and the defendant together and there was no DNA evidence, so the prosecution was relying only on circumstantial evidence—their past childhood connection, the method of the killing, the proximity to the other murders and the nightclub setting like in three other deaths. Wentworth was looking good on this one until Drake started talking about what a fine, upstanding young man the victim was and Bad Penny emerged by saying half under his breath, "yeah right", and rolling his eyes. His annoyance was noticed by the jury and it made him look guilty on that charge as well.

The State's next charge, focusing on the next victim, Monsignor O'Brien, bludgeoned to death with a gold chalice, was most damning. Friction ridges, commonly known as fingerprints, belonging to the defendant, were found on the murder weapon and the defendant's DNA was found mixed in the blood of the Priest's.

An expert testified that the generally accepted minimum number of matching points for a fingerprint match to be bulletproof was twelve and the chalice he examined was a twenty point match, making it, in his words, bombproof. On cross Ben tried the only strategy possible-to question the expert's experience, and training. Turned out he was trained by the FBI and was that agency's top expert in the country and had testified in over two-hundred trials with a greater than ninety-nine per cent conviction rate. It was the only real error Ben made: a rookie mistake, not knowing the answer in advance of a question he asked.

At the end of the afternoon session, they moved to the defense's assigned chamber to debrief. With the uniformed officer again waiting on the other side of the only door, they sat around the conference table. It accommodated just enough castered chairs in dark gray fabric to accommodate the small team. Harsh neon lights of the type found in all government buildings were hard on the eyes. Squinting, Ben said, "Not a good first day, but it's still early. We'll be okay."

Pennington said, "I have a question."

"Shoot," said Ben.

"The word s-e-p-i-a. Is it pronounced sEHpia, or sEEpia?"

Ben glared at Pennington. "It's sEHpia, Pennington, but why in the world is that important right now, pray tell?"

"I've been thinking about it all day. Because everyone should know how to pronounce sepia."

"You've been thinking about it all day. You didn't have anything more important to think about during your trial for multiple murders?"

Then Ben, frustrated with Pennington's lack of interest, said, "Michael, tell the officer he can deliver Pennington back to the jail."

"Will do, boss."

Michael knocked on the door to signal the officer, who entered and cuffed Wentworth for the short trip back to the detention center.

Ben turned to Gerry and glanced at Michael. "How about a glass of wine? Martini? I'm buying."

Gerry said, "I'm in."

Michael, "I need to touch base with my girlfriend, but I can do it."

"Sounds good. Johnny's Hideway, in forty-five minutes?

Said Michael, "Nothing but old people go there."

Ben, an old soul said, "Yeah, but it's the only place in town that plays Sinatra."

***

They arrived at the same time. Getting a table wasn't easy on a Wednesday night, but they managed. When they sat down, Love and Marriage by Sinatra was playing on the sound system. Ben ordered a Tito's Vodka martini shaken. Michael ordered a Maker's Mark Manhattan and Gerry a Cakebread chardonnay. A string of songs by Dean, Tony and Bing followed. After Bing the dj returned to the Italian theme with Andy Williams.

Gerry said, "So what do you think?"

"I thought *I* was going too kill *him* when he rolled his eyes and said "yeah right."

"Yeah, I wanted to go up side his head, myself," said Gerry.

"The only chance we have is if I can convince them he didn't know what he was doing. That his head injury was so bad he didn't know what he was doing was wrong."

Michael tilted his glass toward Ben and said, "Good luck with that."

Gerry said, "Yeah, good luck."

Ben inclined his head and tilted his own glass in return.

After an hour and a quarter, during which time each finished two drinks, Ben announced, "I'm going to make it an early night."

"I'll walk out with you," said Michael.

"Me too." Gerry was a lightweight anyway. Two glasses of wine were one past her self-imposed limit.

In the parking lot Ben called over his shoulder, "You guys be careful."

"You too, boss." Gerry worried about him after the two martinis. It wouldn't look good for the defense attorney in the city's highest profile murder case in thirty years to get a DUI.

***

Ben had to get up earlier than usual to be in court before the judge. Days like this were when his morning routine really annoyed him. Morning constitutional, shave, brush his teeth, shower, dress in his suit, lace shoes, tie his tie with the four-in-hand knot he preferred. That routine took more than an hour. It was the only time he wished he worked on a highway crew and didn't have to dress up or even shower. Then over an hour between walking to the nearest MARTA station and catching the Atlanta transit train to the stop closest to his building, then another hike.

He usually worked on his iPad while riding MARTA, or when he was in the middle of a trial, like today, he'd sit quietly, deep in thought, going over his strategy and rehearsing his lines for the day.

When the train emerged from a tunnel, north of the midtown station, picking up a signal, his cellphone trilled.

"Gerry, talk to me." he said.

"Hey boss. I've just been thinking. Creating doubt might be easier than you think."

"How so?"

'When you present your defense, remember he looked like everyman. He doesn't look that way now, but he did then. And the women in bars, well it wasn't their first time in a bar. They've hung out with other men. Maybe the witnesses won't be quite as sure when you go on the offensive."

The train entered another tunnel and he lost his signal. "Gerry, Gerry?"

***

Ben, once again was the first person in the courtroom, with his team following closely behind. He had stopped at Starbucks and brought himself and his team coffees. Michael's venti Verona with two percent and three splendas, his own with skim milk and two packages of honey. Gerry got a grande, skinny, iced caramel macchiato.

District Attorney Drake and his team of young protégées arrived a moment later and had stopped by the coffee shop in the building, carrying the generic paper cups that looked embarrassed without green Starbucks logos.

"Good morning, Ben. Any interest in talking about a deal? Save the people of the Great State of Georgia some money before this goes too far?"

"No Mr. Drake, I want to see your hole card before I even think about a deal." Ben knew he wasn't interested in saving the people of Georgia money. He obviously wasn't as confident as he was letting on.

"Well, let me know if you change your mind."

Ben didn't respond.

Wentworth entered escorted by the two all-business, spit-shined, uniformed officers.

"Mornin, Counselor," he said, grinning. It was all a show to him.

The bailiff entered bringing the judge's day's refreshments. It reminded one of a rockstar requesting nothing but green m&ms and Perrier in his dressing room before a concert. "All rise. Hear ye, hear ye. The District Court for the City of Atlanta is now in session, the honorable, Judge William Stephens presiding."

Judge Stephens was jaunty with just the peaks of his bow tie barely peeking out above the top of his robe. In his mid-forties, with salt and pepper hair, rumors abounded that he was quite the ladies man. He reminded people of George Clooney, even having the up-to-something grin showing the perfectly straight line of sparkling white crowns.

"If the state is ready, you may call your first witness."

"Thank you, your honor." Mr. Drake called the bartender from Tongue & Groove who served Pennington and victim number five, Miss Watson.

The bailiff swore him in. "State your name, please."

"Brandon Parker."

"Do you swear to tell the truth, the whole truth and nothing but the truth?

"I do."

The district attorney approached the witness stand. "Mr. Parker, would you please recount for the jury the scene as you remember it the night Miss Watson was murdered?

"Yes sir. I was working behind the main bar, we have three at T&G, and the defendant, Wentworth, sat down. He ordered a jack-and-coke. I recall him asking me when the crowd would pick up, something to that effect. I told him it would get better after midnight. He swore when I told him that. It wasn't long after that that Miss Watson sat down at the bar. I could tell he was interested in her."

"Had you seen Miss Watson before?"

"Yes. I would describe her as a semi-regular. Maybe came in every two or three weeks. Weekends only. Certainly someone who had better things to do than hang out in a bar every night. She was classy, not out to hook up."

"Sorry to interrupt. Please go back. You could tell he was interested in her?"

"Yeah he was feeding her a line of crap like all guys do. Only, this was different. It sounded like he was making it up on the fly."

"Give us an example."

"He told her he was named for his great-grandfather, a civil war hero, and that he was a bodyguard. I believe he called it personal protection."

"Personal protection?" Jonathan Drake turned and glared at the defendant.

Wentworth looked away, under the pressure of the powerful stare, not meaning to, but toward the jury, and rolled his eyes. Ben noticed and loudly cleared his throat to remind Pennington to control his emotions.

"So listening to him, what was your conclusion?"

Ben spoke. "Object, your honor. Asking the witness to draw a conclusion."

The judge: "We all know it's his opinion. Overruled."

"My conclusion was, he was, pardon my French, full of shit."

"Then what happened?"

He bought her a drink, a cosmopolitan, and after she finished it they left together."

The DA then presented the collected DNA evidence taken from the neck, in the ligature marks, from the defendant. Damning evidence.

"No further questions, your honor. Your witness," he said to Ben.

"Mr. Parker, how many men that you encounter in your line of work do you think are, as you so colorfully put it, full of shit, pardon *my* French.

"All of them."

"All of them. That's all, your honor."

No major bombshells were being exploded by either side, but the prosecution was slowly, methodically, building an ironclad case against the defendant.

During a bathroom break before the next witness, Wentworth went to the restroom and knocked out one hundred pushups on the filthy floor.

The next count was of first degree murder in the death of number six, barber, Robert Bowden. Again the physical evidence was overwhelming. The police crime scene investigator testified that Wentworth's hair and dead skin, from his haircut, containing DNA evidence, was on the cape and on the chair where Mr. Bowden's body was found. Remembering how frustrated he was at listening to the barber pratter, Bad Penny surfaced again and shrugged at Ben Wasserman. A gesture of what-can-I-say? It was all Ben could do to control his own emotions in front of the jury.

Nearing four-thirty pm, calling an end to the day's testimony, the judge said, "We'll resume at nine o'clock tomorrow morning." Banged his gavel, and said, "Dismissed."

***

Friday morning and Ben knew Jonathan Drake would try and wrap up his case before the weekend. The bailiff entered and went through his usual start of day routine. The judge entered, poured a glass of water and unwrapped four peppermints. Popped one in his mouth and lined up the other three.

Tess Chu was the last victim and The DA called the bartender at the Atlanta Hilton as his first witness.

"Would you state your name please?"

"Colleen Anderson."

Ms. Anderson swore to tell the truth, the whole truth and nothing but the truth and then testified that Wentworth bought the victim a drink and asked Ms. Anderson to send it to her.

"What happened then?" the DA asked.

"After they finished their drinks Miss Chu left for a few minutes, then the defendant went to the restroom, while she was gone, then after Miss Chu returned, they left together."

He then called Beverly Bowen, the waitress at the Polaris rooftop lounge at the Hyatt Regency to testify.

She testified that Wentworth and Miss Chu had a couple of drinks, but while Miss Chu was in the restroom, Wentworth told her to bring him a plain Coca-Cola for his second drink. She thought it odd because she felt like he didn't want Miss Chu to know. After their second round they left together.

When she had finished, Jonathan Drake said, "Your honor, the state rests its case."

"Thank you, then this court will recess until Monday morning at nine o'clock, at which time the defense will rebut."

Ben stood along with Pennington and said, "Thank you, your honor."

Bad Penny said, "I'll be back in time for dinner. How about that. Have a good weekend, Counselor. I guess I'll be having fucking fish for dinner again. Goddamn Catholics have their hands in everything."

"You too, Pennington. Survive until Monday."

Gerry, Michael and Ben said their good-byes and extended their wishes for a good weekend.

The uniformed policemen cuffed Wentworth and escorted him out while Ben shook hands with Mr. Drake.

***

Bad Penny was delivered to the detention center. Went straight to the cafeteria. "How about some goddamn dinner," then looking at the pans, "fucking fish again? Don't bother. I'll just go to bed early tonight."

Went to his cell. Got undressed and yelled to no one in particular, but one of the guards. "I need this fucking suit cleaned. I can't go to court Monday in a fucking stinky suit."

***

Saturday afternoon he went to a small common room that held vinyl sofas, with a small widescreen television protected by a plastic screen cover. Several inmates sprawled on the couches, arms and legs akimbo watching the New York Yankees play the Boston Red Sox. There were fans of both teams but since Bad Penny had never seen either team play before he didn't care who won. It was just a way to be out of his goddamn cell.

***

Monday morning started Ben's show. Same as the week before, he arrived first. Then the rest of his team and the prosecution team.

Even though he was cuffed, Bad Penny looked like he was making a grand entrance when he arrived. Grinning and looking around, making eye contact with anyone who glanced his way. Giving a thumbs up to the gallery while flashing the most insincere smile he could muster was a little over the top. Enjoying what he considered rockstar status.

He shook hands with Ben and said, "Knock 'em dead, counselor. Oh, wait…that's what I do." He put his hand on Ben's shoulder, real buddy-buddy like and said, "I crack myself up."

Judge William Stephens entered.

The bailiff: "All rise. This court is in session."

"The defense calls Dr. Jason Pierce." The emergency room doctor who first saw Wentworth.

He was sworn in and took the witness stand. He described a TBI, a traumatic brain injury, telling the court the defendant's injury when he arrived in the emergency room was a fractured skull over the left frontal lobe, the section of the brain that controls all behavior, likes, dislikes, personality and everything that makes people themselves

"So, someone could become a completely different person, unrecognizable to their closest friends, their families, even to themselves?" Mr. Wasserman was taking a path that surprised even himself.

"That's correct. It's conceivable that someone could even forget who they were prior to such an injury."

"Thank you Doctor Pierce. That will be all."

Not looking up from his notes, Jonathan Drake said, "No questions, your honor.

"The defense calls Doctor Jacob Watters."

He was sworn in and Mr. Wasserman asked him, "Doctor Watters would you please tell us about your experience with Mr. Wentworth?

"I was Mr. Wentworth's internist for a two-week period after he left the ER and was assigned to a room."

"What can you tell us about his stay under your care?"

"The first thing we had to do was perform brain surgery. We have a neurosurgeon, Doctor Warren Dunham on call to perform emergency surgeries."

"And how did it go?"

"It was uneventful. There was blood pooling in the brain that had to be evacuated. I mean anytime you have to do brain surgery you have concerns, but it was textbook."

"Then what happened."

"He was unconscious for almost two weeks. When he finally awoke, he was confused, disoriented. A very normal condition."

"How so? How was he disoriented and confused?"

"He didn't know why he was in a hospital room, or how he got there and couldn't remember what had happened to put him there."

"Then what"

"He got very angry, angry at just about everything I told him when I answered his questions."

"Is that typical?"

"Typical? No. Most people, after a brain injury, and when they're confused, they get scared and emotional. Crying is common. And Wentworth didn't appear to be scared. He seemed to be incensed at everyone, me, the nurses, staff, everyone."

"Thank you Doctor. That will be all."

"The defense calls Miss Ashley Denson."

Miss Denson took the stand.

"Miss Denson, how long have you know Mr. Wentworth?"

"Since college. We met junior year at Georgia Tech University, so that would be about fifteen years."

"And you've remained close that entire time?"

"Yes, friends."

"So you've never been romantically involved?"

Unable to remember Ashley and thinking she looked hot, Pennington winked at her and then gave her a naughty grin. Fortunately for him, none of the jury members seemed to notice his inappropriate behavior.

"With Pennington? Heavens no. We've never looked at each other that way."

Upon hearing her say that, Pennington gave her a look of irritation, this one noticed by at least two jurors.

"You know he's unable to remember your relationship."

"That's what I understand."

"So, can you tell us about seeing him for the first time after the accident?

"Yes, he called me and wanted me to pick him up at Grady."

"And how did he seem to you?"

"Why, he was horrible, swearing, angry. I'd never heard him use that kind of language, not even once in all those years."

"And what did you do?"

"When I got off work that afternoon I drove downtown and picked him up."

"And how did that go?"

"Terribly. When I got to his room, he cursed me for being late. I wasn't late," she lamented. "Anyone from Atlanta knows Friday afternoon traffic is horrendous." The gallery squirmed in their seats and smothered their chuckles with their hands at that comment.

"And then what?"

"I asked him if he wanted to stop for dinner, a salad, or sushi, the kind of food he had always eaten, and he said he wanted a G-D hamburger. I'd never seen him eat red meat, ever. Then I asked him if he wanted to stop by and see his hair stylist. He looked a wee bit ragged after his hospital stay. He said he was going to let his hair grow out and grow a beard. That wasn't the Pennington I knew. He's always been so well groomed and cultured."

That will be all for this witness, your honor."

Ben Wasserman had spent Monday calling a host of friends, bartenders and barristas, all who gave testimony about his effeminate pacifism prior to his brain injury, in sharp contrast to his behavior post-TBI. It was clear to all that Pennington Wentworth was a different person due to the injury.

The witnesses' testimony had taken most of the day.

"This court will recess until 9:00 in the morning." Judge Stephens banged his gavel.

***

On Tuesday, Judge Stephens gave the jury their instructions. That they were to return a verdict of guilty or not guilty on each of the seven counts and could not decide on a lesser charge.

When the jury left, Ben told the officers to return Pennington to the detention center. He didn't expect to see a verdict returned anytime soon.

Wednesday morning the jury sent a note to the judge asking to see a transcript of the testimony regarding the murder of Mark Spalding.

The murder of Mark Spalding was the only one in which there was no physical evidence and no witnesses connecting Wentworth to the defendant. The jury was unable to agree on a verdict.

One juror, a studious looking man in his forties, was adamant. "Just because the defendant knew Spalding—we can't… I mean, I'll be damned if I'll vote to convict on that."

"A woman in her fifties, a small technology business owner was just as convinced of his guilt. "They knew each other. He was murdered violently like the others. It happened after he left a nightclub like the first one. The circumstantial evidence is more than enough for me."

The jury took a vote to see where thy stood. Eleven for conviction, one against. The rest of the day was spent debating among themselves. A poll before five o'clock revealed that two others had changed sides putting them even farther apart. What they all could agree on was that they felt that in all the charges the defendant knew the difference between right and wrong even if he did have a brain injury.

They sent word to the judge of their stalemate but agreed to keep trying the next morning.

***

The bailiff called Ben to notify him of the ongoing impasse.

Ben told Michael and Gerry about the bailiff's call. "I'm not excited about it because I'm guessing they're just hung up on one of the charges. In fact I'll bet you a drink I know which one."

"I'll take that bet boss," Gerry said. "Which one?"

"The Spalding murder. They obviously want DNA evidence or a witness putting them together. Which will mean that's the only charge they return for not guilty. Dammit"

"You don't know that. Don't give up yet boss." Gerry was pleading with the man she had so much respect for.

"Yeah, boss. It's not over until the fat lady sings."

"Yeah, but she's warming up, Michael."

Ben had begun to think that he and his team of young Turks, which is the way he liked to think of them, were unbeatable, but it looked like this time they'd bitten off more than they could chew.

***

Thursday morning dawned with a heavy summer rain, the kind that might not last long but would leave a gray blanket of dread hanging over Atlanta all day. Ben called the detention center and since he anticipated a verdict this morning told the supervisor on duty that he should probably have Wentworth delivered to the courthouse.

When Pennington arrived, he was more subdued with his entrance since he'd been chastised by Ben about the previous one.

Ben motioned for the officers to take Pennington to the small conference room in which they'd eaten lunch.

Inside the room, Ben said, "Pennington, I'm sorry but I think you should prepare yourself for guilty verdicts." Ben looked like he was tearing up.

Bad Penny resurfaced, clapped the defense attorney on the shoulder. "Counselor, you still don't get it. I...don't...give...a...shit."

"Well I do, Pennington. We'll appeal. I'll get you in that institution yet."

"No...no...no...Counselor...Ben, I'd rather be dead than live with a bunch of crazies.

Just before noon, the bailiff was summoned to the the jury room. They informed him that they had reached verdicts. He notified Judge Stephens and the court session was called.

The jury was escorted in.

The bailiff said, "Court is in session."

The judge banged his gavel. Ben Wasserman and Pennington Wentworth, II stood.

"Members of the jury, have you reached a verdict?"

"The foreman rose. "We have, your honor."

"On the first count of Manslaughter in the death of John Matthews, how do you find?"

"We find the defendant guilty."

He read the charges of first degree murder and the victim's name for all seven counts.

Ben won his bet. Guilty on all but count number three, the murder of Mark Spalding.

"The court will recess until nine o'clock tomorrow when I will inform you of the sentence."

Bad Pennington said, "So, that's that. What do you think the sentence will be counselor?"

"The judge can decide, at his discretion, to sentence you to be executed, or sentence you to life without parole, in which case, the state of Georgia will make the decision about execution or not, at some later point."

"Aiight."

"But don't forget, Savannah gets their shot at you now."

"Shit. That's a waste of the goddamn taxpayers' money."

***

"Court is now in session." There was no one to swear in since the only thing on the agenda was for Judge Stephens to hand down his decision.

Ben and Pennington stood.

"I can, at my discretion, Mr. Wentworth, sentence you to be executed, or leave that, deadly serious decision to be made by someone else. So with the power given to me by the state of Georgia, due to your callous disregard for human life and your actions in this courtroom, I will exercise my authority and sentence you to be executed at a time and date to be determined by the state.

It appeared that Bad Penny had a hint of a grin on his face at that moment.

Chapter 18
The Second Trial

Bad Penny's new found status as a convicted murderer increased his prestige at the detention center. Now he was a certified badass. All ethnic groups gave him his props and gave him a wide path when he walked by. It only lasted two days before he got a change of address.

The state of Georgia sent a van to transport Wentworth to the Georgia Diagnostic and Classification Prison. Since he was now a convicted murderer, he would be held there during his trial in Savannah and until a date was set for his execution. The prison, the largest in the state, held a maximum of two-thousand, three hundred inmates in eight cell blocks consisting of double-bunked and single-bunked cells and eight dormitories. It also held a medical unit. In addition to being the central hub for all inmates entering the state of Georgia's prison system, it also housed all male death row inmates and was where the executions were carried out. As in a majority of states, Georgia used lethal injection and they were carried out in a separate building called appropriately, the Death House. The "house" was a single-entrance fortified building accessed only through the prison yard. The actual execution room was approximately 8x12 feet and decorated with only a gurney outfitted with white sheets and a pillow. Directly on the front wall of the execution room was a large window into the observation room, where witnesses would sit on three long wooden benches for viewing. On the opposite side of the execution room was another window into a private viewing room where the warden, executioners and authorized personnel oversaw the administering of the lethal injections.

The GDCP was a little over an hour from the Atlanta Detention Center. "Can't you son of a bitches drive this bucket any fucking faster? I got somewhere I gotta be." He was not going to let them think they could get the best of him.

The van passed through the chain link fenced double gate, topped with razor wire and a hundred yards further, backed up to the double doors at the rear of the prison. And just in case anybody was watching, he strutted as he entered the rear entrance to the facility. Had to make a good first impression.

Bad Penny's paperwork was processed completing the transfer and he was officially the responsibility of the state of Georgia.

He asked the uniformed guard processing him, "You know I haven't eaten since last night's supper. When can I get some god damn lunch, or a fucking snack, or something?"

The guard was disinterested. "Feeding you isn't my responsibility."

"Well, whose fucking responsibility is it?"

"Not mine. That's all that matters," said while he focused, or pretended to focus on the paperwork in front of him.

The next two days would be occupied with psychological, medical and mental tests and diagnostics. First, though, he was escorted to his cell, his new home for the foreseeable future. As he strutted down the cellblock, the hardcore, long-serving inmates weren't impressed with Bad Penny. These were the hardest of the hard, Georgia's most incorrigible. Unrepentant murderers, rapists and kidnappers, all of them trying to get over on someone.

The catcalls, whistles and taunts started again, just like the first time he walked down the cell block at the City of Atlanta Detention Center. Unlike the first time however, Bad Penny wasn't intimidated in the least. The first time he had to fake it. But not this time. "Bring it on, you fuckers," he shouted.

The cell door was opened by a guard in a control room. As Bad Penny entered he said to the guard escorting him, "I'm about to starve to fucking death. How do I get some goddamn lunch around here?"

"Ah, let's see." 'In an exaggerated movement designed to aggravate Wentworth, the guard slowly lifted his left arm to steal a glance at his watch. "Eleven forty-five—in fifteen minutes you'll see guards appear in the cell block, the cell doors will open automatically and all you losers will be escorted to the cafeteria. How does that work for you?"

"Just make sure they're not late."

***

The guards showed up a few minutes later. A buzzer sounded and all the cell doors opened at once on each of the block's two levels.

Bad Penny yelled, "It's about fucking time."

And from the upper level, a chorus of, "Yeah, it's about fucking time."

As they were herded into the cafeteria they grouped together ethnically like in every prison in the country.

To the servers. "I want three goddamn hamburgers. I need some fucking protein."

Bad Penny sat with some hardcore-looking caucasians. He removed the buns from two of the burgers and stacked all three slabs of beef on one bun.

"How ya doin?" the one to his right said.

"Aiight."

"Rookie?"

"Just got here."

"Why you here?'

"Sons of bitches convicted me of six killings in the ATL."

"DP?"

"Yep."

"Figures. Six. Shit."

"Got off on one. And they haven't even tried me for the five in Savannah yet."

Again, "Shit. I'm Joe." He extended his right hand.

Bad Penny grasped it in a manly clench and said, "Penny...Bad Penny."

"I get it. You bad, all right What's that, twelve killings?

Bad Penny stuck out his chest. Played it cool. "I think so. Math wasn't my best subject." Truth was he didn't remember what his best subject was...or his worst.

After lunch they got their time in the prison yard. That made Bad Penny feel better. He hadn't been regular with his workouts while the trial was going on. He had an hour in the yard and did five hundred pushups and five hundred bodyweight squats. After finishing with those he claimed the pull up bar and the last thing he did was knock out fifty chin-ups. He had to keep working out even if he was going to be executed because he couldn't let those sons-of-bitches fuck with his head. He'd show all those motherfuckers that he would beat them. He'd never give in. He'd be working out the day they stuck the needle into his vein. He wanted the executioner to say, "best vein I've ever seen," due to his vascularity from working out so hard.

The next day he was called to the warden's office, Mr. Jackson.

Mr. Jackson was in his fifties, his old-style haircut and black horn-rimmed glasses made him look at least a decade older, like he was from a different era, a man in *his* fifties, stuck, in *the* fifties.

He was escorted into the anteroom and sat. A moment later, the warden's secretary told him he could enter.

The warden, an affable man, gestured for him to sit.

Coming around his desk, he extended his hand and said, "Mr. Wentworth."

"Warden.

"Your trial in Savannah will start next Tuesday at nine o'clock. You'll will depart by one of our vans, escorted by three armed guards every morning at six a.m. But I suspect you won't have to do that for very long. I suspect it will be a short trial. Done inside of a week."

"Aiight."

Bad Penny figured the warden was right. The second trial probably wouldn't even last as long as the first.

***

The guard who escorted him to see the warden returned for him and took him to a small room and told him to sit at a white formica-topped table a little larger than a card table. A moment after he sat down a man, early seventies, six feet tall, balding, twenty pounds overweight, entered. "James Andrews, your attorney. Court-appointed, of course. Course you'll be paying my fee out of your assets. I understand you're flush."

"I reviewed the transcripts of your trial in Atlanta and I've studied the case against you in Savannah. I think your previous attorney was onto something, headed in the right direction, but I plan on doing it better."

"Aiight."

"I don't need anything from you. Just show up on time and come dressed to play."

***

Due to the two meetings, Bad Penny was late getting to lunch.

Joe had held a seat for him. Center stage in front of an admiring posse of white guys. Tats, goatees, muscles and piercings. Joe had told them about Bad Penny and his reputation was growing. It was just what he wanted, a serial killer's rep. And the respect that came with it.

Joe spoke To the group. "I've told you about him. This is Bad Penny."

A chorus of "How ya doins" echoed around the long table.

Talking as cons will, he told them how he'd killed twelve people, without having to embellish. Even among hardened criminals, their wide-eyed silence showed they were impressed. Serial killers *were* the rock stars of prisons.

***

Bad Penny was escorted to the prison van and along with three uniformed guards, it pulled away from the Georgia Diagnostic and Classification Prison at six o'clock on Tuesday morning. He was dressed in the same suit that Ben Wasserman had bought for him while he was in the City of Atlanta Detention Center. The driver would have to put the pedal to the metal to reach the Chatham County Criminal Building by nine o'clock.

Typical of convicts who spend most of their unoccupied time asleep, he was snoring within fifteen minutes.

About halfway between Macon, GA and Savannah, the driver left I-16 at the Metter, GA exit and pulled into a Burger King parking lot and drove to the line to the pickup window. After getting various types of biscuits with eggs and sausages with coffee for themselves, one of the guards passed Bad Penny a cup of black coffee and said,

"You should consider yourself lucky."

Under his breath. "Aiight, son-of-bitch."

What'd you say?"

"I said, consider myself lucky for a fucking cup of black coffee?"

"You know, this is the exit for Reidsville State Prison. I used to work there before they transferred me to the big dog," the one riding shotgun said.

The one driving said, "Yeah, I've seen that place. That's one shitty facility."

"Yeah, it looks like a crappy small town airport building."

"It's bad enough having to work there. I can't imagine being imprisoned there for years.

The sounds of chewing replaced the sounds of talking for the next quarter hour.

***

The Court Building was an ugly, six story, post-modern structure designed for function only and not for aesthetic appeal. Pulled up to the guard's booth at the entrance to the parking lot and after he raised the gate arm they were allowed to enter.

***

His attorney, James Andrews, was waiting for him when he arrived and with his seersucker suit reminiscent of Matlock's on the old hit television show, rumpled like it was, and red nose and yellowed whites of his eyes, he looked like he'd had bourbon for breakfast. He was an old school lawyer and in fact got his law degree in a time when the state of Georgia didn't require an undergraduate degree to go to law school.

"David Vardaman, an Assistant District Attorney is prosecuting. They must be pretty sure of themselves, didn't send the DA, himself. Well. That's okay. I've got a thing or two to show them." The ADA was young, looked a little younger than Wentworth himself.

The charge was first degree murder in each of the deaths.

The bailiff entered just before nine o'clock and poured the judge a glass of water and set the pitcher down.

Taking his place and standing at attention, he waited for Judge Marvin Burkett to enter from his chambers. Judge Burkett, a large African American man, looked jovial, but he was all business in the courtroom.

"All rise. This court is now in session.

Judge Burkett asked, "is the state prepared to present its case?"

Taking them in order of the deaths, the state started with the death of Miss Hartman.

"It is your honor. The state calls Joy Burke."

Miss Burke was twenty-two years old, pretty, with baby fine blonde hair.

"State your full name for the record."

"Joy Denise Burke."

"Do you swear to tell the truth, the whole truth and nothing but the truth?"

"I do."

Miss Burke, were you working at the Coffee Fox on the morning Anette Hartman was there, the day she died?"

"Yes, sir."

"Can you please tell the court what transpired, as you remember it?"

"Miss Hartman came in between 9:45 and 10:00. She was a regular so I knew her well enough to be able to tell that something was bothering her, but I didn't press. She ordered her usual, a caramel macchiato, and went over to sit on a sofa. She was there for maybe forty-five minutes before a guy came in, got a large black coffee and sat down near her. I couldn't hear what they were talking about but I could see she got even more agitated. After he finished his coffee they left together. When I got home from work I heard about her death on the news. The report said the police thought it was an accident but remembering him," she pointed at the defendant, "I was afraid he'd done something to her. I mean look at him. Ugh."

Andrews stood. "I object, your honor. Opinion."

"Sustained."

"No other questions, your honor."

The judge asked Mr. Andrews. "Do you have any questions for this witness?

"Yes, your honor. Miss Burke, did you see the defendant do anything wrong?"

"See anything? No, it was just a feeling."

"A feeling? Do you have an education in psychology, Miss Burke?"

"Three hours, in college."

"So, one class. That's all, your honor."

"Court will recess until 1:30."

Mr. Andrews turned to his client and asked, "Pennington, do you want lunch?"

"I could eat a burger."

"Sam," he said to his gofer, "Go get us up some Whoppers." He gave him a couple of twenties.

"Make mine a double Whopper with cheese." Pennington shrugged. "I need the god damn protein."

Sam returned with the large burgers. Bad Penny inhaled his double.

Mr. Andrews said, "So Pennington, where'd you go to school?"

"They tell me I went to Georgia Tech."

"What'd you study?"

"You can probably find out. When you do, you tell me."

They finished their lunch and returned to the courtroom. Judge Burkett returned. "All rise. This court is back in session."

To the ADA the judge said, "You may call your next witness."

"The state calls Vince Milsap." Vince was a bartender at Jazz'd.

"Mr. Milsap, were you working behind the bar the night the two gentleman were found murdered after leaving Jazz'd?"

"Yes, sir."

"What do you remember about that night?"

"The defendant was sitting at the bar, minding his own business. He didn't fit in. Wasn't dressed well enough to be there. We have pretty high class customers. Anyway, two guys, obviously gay, sat at the bar too. He's trying to ignore them, but one of them bought him a drink. He tells me, I didn't buy this. I said he did, nodding my head at the guy who sent it over. The next thing I know the three of them are leaving together."

"Let me make sure I've got it. One of the deceased bought the defendant a drink and then you saw them leave together?'

'That's correct.'

"Oh, and what time was that?"

"It was almost midnight when they left."

"Thank you. That will be all for this witness, your honor."

"You may step down."

'The state calls Dr. Houston Shipley."

Dr. Shipley was sworn in.

"What is your position, Dr. Shipley?"

"I'm a medical doctor, an internist, with a specialty in forensics and I work for the Savannah Police Department as a forensics specialist."

"Thank you, Dr. Shipley, and did you examine the bodies of Wayne Mitchell and Curtis Burns?"

"I did."

"And were you able to determine the time of death?"

"According to body temperature, and the lividity, I calculated the time of death to be between midnight and one o'clock a.m.

"So according to witness testimony, no more than one hour after the victims left Jazz'd with the defendant." There was no question.

"Your honor, that's all I have for this witness."

"The defense has no questions, your honor."

"You may step down, Doctor."

"Your honor, the state will move on to the next charge against the defendant."

"Then this court will recess until 9 o'clock tomorrow morning. Court is adjourned." The banging of Judge Burkett's gavel startled Bad Penny just as he was falling asleep.

***

Since court adjourned about three-thirty, the prison van was able to return Wentworth to the Georgia Diagnostic and Classification Prison in time for the evening meal. He changed into his prison orange in the back of the van as they drove. He was taken directly to the cafeteria and after the prisoner applause for him died down, he told the server, "I want three fucking hamburgers." Still convinced of his need to work out and build more muscle, he was going to eat beef three times a day if he could get it. What he didn't know was he hadn't eaten meat in close to twenty years and this was one of the most obvious examples of his brain and personality change.

He slept fitfully, possibly an acknowledgement and recognition of his impending execution. Retrieving him from his cell at five-forty a.m. they repeated the previous days sequence of events to get him to court in time.

Driving through the Burger King in Metter, GA again, this time he was able to talk the driver into ordering him two steak biscuits to go with his black coffee. The Georgia Department of Corrections credit card the guard used would get a workout if this trial went longer than expected.

The driver blindly tossed Bad Penny his breakfast sandwiches over his shoulder landing them in his lap, where he sat in the back seat.

***

They made it with fifteen minutes to spare.

"Mornin', counselor, how you feelin?"

"I'm fine, Pennington, fine. But, Pennington, I've got to tell you. It's not looking too good."

"Well counselor, I'll tell you like I told Mr. Wasserman—that was my attorney in Atlanta—I really don't give a flying fuck.

His attorney didn't know how to respond to that and just shook his head. He'd never had a client who acted like he truly didn't care if he lived or died. And if he himself could testify, he would because he felt that that was proof of his client's impaired mental state.

The bailiff entered and went through his routine of catering to the judge's needs. The judge entered.

"All rise."

"Court is now in session."

"In the charges of first degree murder in the deaths of Mary Bishop and Thomas Singleton, the state calls Dr. Houston Shipley."

He approached the stand and the judge said, "You're still under oath, Dr. Shipley."

"Dr. Shipley, did you examine the bodies of Mary Bishop and Thomas Singleton?"

"I did."

"And what did you find?"

"There was semen on both bodies."

"Did you examine it and what did you find?'

"I did examine the semen and it was a perfect DNA match to the sample I took from the defendant."

"When you say a perfect match what does that mean, scientifically?"

"It's a one in four billion chance that it belonged to the defendant."

"So fewer than two people on the planet could have produced that DNA?"

"That's correct."

"Your honor, the state rests its case."

"Does the defense have questions for this witness?"

"No, your honor."

'The court will recess until one-thirty when the defense can present its case.

***

The judge entered to a refilled courtroom.

"All rise. Court is now in session." A blanket of quiet descended over the gallery.

"Mr. Andrews, you may open."

"The defense calls Ashley Denson."

The bailiff: "Do you swear to tell the truth, the whole truth and nothing but the truth?"

"I do."

"Miss Denson, would you describe for the court, your relationship with Mr. Wentworth?"

"Pennington and I have been friends since our junior year at Georgia Tech."

"Friends? No romantic involvement?"

"Heavens no. We didn't look at each other that way. We're like brother and sister, with the same dynamics as real siblings."

"I see. And what can you tell us about his demeanor?'

"Pennington has always been the sweetest, kindest, gentlest soul you'd ever want to meet."

"And you picked him up at Grady Hospital after his car accident and head injury. Can you tell the court what happened?"

"He called me first thing that morning and he was so profane, just positively foul-mouthed. I didn't think he even knew words like that. And he was so impatient. I work, and he wanted me to drop what I was doing and pick him up right then. When I did get there, he was furious. I thought he'd be grateful, but no."

Even though, due to the hot early summer day, the air conditioning was running full blast, Bad Penny, in what was most likely an acknowledgement of his impending fate, was covered with a film of slick, sour sweat, sour with the smell of fear.

"Thank you. That's all I have for this witness, your honor."

"You may call your next witness."

"The state calls Dr. Jason Pierce to the stand."

Dr. Pierce was sworn in.

"Dr. Pierce, will you tell the court where you work and what you do?"

"I'm an emergency room physician at Grady Memorial Hospital in Atlanta."

"And were you on duty the night Pennington Wentworth, II was admitted?"

"Yes."

"What can you tell us about his condition?"

"Mr. Wentworth had a large contusion and swelling over the frontal lobe, er…the front of his head. He was observed as being glassy-eyed, incoherent and in and out of consciousness. I ordered a CT scan and it revealed an epidural hematoma, a large collection of blood over one hemisphere of the brain. His condition resulted in internal bleeding with blood in the stomach causing him to produce bloody vomit. He needed immediate neurological surgery to evacuate the hemorrhage.

"Based on your experience what did you expect from his injuries?"

"Having seen this condition a number of times, I expected, and even told a nurse, that he was guaranteed to have psychological problems, personality change, problems with argumentativeness and aggression."

"Another question, Dr. Pierce, would someone in Pennington's condition be able to discern whether or not his actions were good or bad, would he know the difference in right and wrong."

"In the case of Mr. Wentworth, in my opinion, he would not know the difference."

"No further questions, your honor."

The ADA: "Cross, your honor."

"Proceed."

"Doctor, was it guaranteed? 100% positive he'd have these issues?"

"100%? No, but…"

"That's all.

"Re-examine, your honor."

"But what, Doctor?"

"I was going to say I'd never seen anyone who hadn't had problems after this kind of injury."

"Thank you. That's all for this witness, your honor."

"Call your next witness."

"The defense calls Doctor Jacob Watters."

Doctor Watters was seated and sworn in.

"Doctor, what is your position?"

"I'm a staff internist at Grady Memorial."

"And Mr. Wentworth was under your care?"

"Yes, for almost two weeks, while he was hospitalized, I was his primary physician."

"What was your experience with Mr. Wentworth?"

"The patient was angry, argumentative, disputatious and arrogant; and many of our staff were reluctant to be alone with him.

"Dr. Watters, were you surprised by his behavior?"

"Surprised, no. Disappointed. You always have hope that something like this won't result.

Thank you, Dr. Watters. That's all, your honor."

"It's almost five o'clock. We'll recess until tomorrow morning at nine."

***

"I want three god damn hamburgers." Bad Penny was into a routine. As much beef as he could eat, three meals a day. And working out every spare minute he had. It had become an obsession for him.

***

Judge Burkett entered.

"All rise."

The judge banged his gavel. "Court is now in session. The defense may continue."

"The defense has no more witnesses, your honor."

"Then the prosecution may close."

David Vardaman said, "Ladies and gentlemen, the defense has posed a lot of questions Did an evil creature commit these horrendous crimes? When was he born, created? I believe Pennington Wentworth, the second, committed the crimes, because I believe he knew what he was doing was wrong. The evidence speaks for itself. You must return a verdict of guilty on all counts."

The Judge: The defense may make its closing statement.

"Ladies and gentlemen of the jury. Mr. Wentworth is accused of terrible crimes. We all agree on that. What we disagree on is who did it. I believe that someone different, someone evil, someone that didn't even exist before a brain injury, committed those horrendous crimes. I believe that evil creature sits before you today. We have presented evidence by the friend that knew him best and by the doctors that treated him, of a different young man before his obvious brain damage and the evil that resulted due to the brain injury. I believe he needs help. He needs to be in an institution that can help him, take care of him, for the rest of his life. If you agree, find him not guilty of the charges he is accused of, due to mental defect.

Judge Burkett sent the jury away with their instructions. A vote of guilty or not guilty on each account.

"Court is still in session."

Wentworth's attorney decided they should stay close. What he said was, "If I can read a jury, and I can, been doing it almost fifty years— they'll be back in an hour and a half. How about some lunch?" He sent his gofer out to a deli. "I need a big salad. My wife will get mad at me if I eat bad. Don't want that. The little lady's been bitchin' at me for over forty years. I'm about to get tired of it," he said with a mischievous grin.

"What do you want Pennington?"

"How about a burger? The biggest goddamn burger they have, with chili. I can use the extra protein."

"You heard the man. Get him the biggest-ass chili burger they have," he said as he pulled out a Ben Franklin.

He handed the hundred to his gofer and said "Get yourself whatever you want."

They waited in the small conference room assigned to them, for the gopher to return with their lunches.

***

It took longer than the hour-and-a-half Andrews thought, but not by much. While eating their lunch a uniformed security guard entered the room and handed him a note that said the jury was returning.

"Let's do it then," he said.

After the defense sat the jury started filing in.

"Have you reached a verdict," Judge Burkett asked.

The foreman stood. "We have, your honor."

"On the first count of murder in the first degree, how do you find?"

"We find the defendant guilty, your honor."

On the second count of murder in the first degree, how do you find?"

"We find the defendant guilty, your honor."

"On the third count of murder in the first degree, how do you find?"

"We find the defendant guilty, you honor."

It was the same on the fourth and fifth counts.

The jurors were polled individually and each confirmed the verdict the foreman had presented.

Andrews looked beaten. "I'm sorry Pennington. I thought we'd get them."

"Like I told you, counselor. I don't give a shit. I don't think I could live with a bunch of fucking retards anyway. Besides, they can't kill me twice."

Chapter 19 Waiting For Death

Bad Penny was settling back into his prison routine and waiting to find out when he would be executed.

As it turned out he didn't have to wait long.

He was summoned to the warden's office.

"Wentworth."

"Warden."

"We have a date."

"Aiight."

"August fifteenth."

"Less than a month."

"Less than a month."

Bad Penny went to lunch with the rest of the cell block. Told the server. "I want three fucking burgers."

"Yeah, yeah, yeah. I know what you want. The same damn thing you've wanted every meal since you got here."

"Well, fuck you. You're so goddamn smart."

"Well, fuck you."

He went to sit at the table with Joe and his usual crew.

"Hey, how you doin, Penny?"

"I'm aiight."

"What's the matter? You don't seem yourself."

"Nothing really. I got a date."

"No shit? When?"

"Less than a month. August fifteenth."

No shit. They must want to stick a needle in your sorry ass bad.

"Yeah, I guess they do. "

Bad Penny finished eating. "Well I need to go get a workout."

"What for? They gonna kill your ass, man."

"What if they change their mind. I got to keep working out."

"Then keep on, bro. Show 'em they can't wear you down."

Bad Penny went to the prison yard with the others from his cell block. Started with pushups. Half way through his ten sets of one-hundred, he realized he could see the rear drive leading to the entrance to the facility. The movement that caught his attention was a state of Georgia prison bus. It stopped at the rear entrance and momentarily, moving slowly, due to nerves, fright or resigned acceptance, a group of twelve newbies trudged off and toward the entrance to be checked in.

Bad Penny finished five more sets of one-hundred pushups and then started on his one thousand bodyweight squats. He could now do the entire thousand in one set. His hour in the yard was almost up but he knew he could do a hundred pull ups before the horn sounded signaling their return to the cellblock.

The next part of his routine would be a nap before dinner.

***

At the evening meal he asked for his usual "three fucking burgers," and was told there weren't any hamburgers. They had chicken tonight.

"Well shit," he said, "give me some goddamn yardbird, then."

He saw a couple of the newbies with their trays piled high with food nervously looking for a place to sit. He nodded at two chairs next to him indicating that it would be okay for them to sit there.

"Thanks," one of them said.

"Yeah, thanks," said the other.

"No prob." They looked scared to death. He could smell the odor of fear in their sweat. Bad Penny was sure he hadn't been that scared when he walked into the Atlanta Detention Center.

Bad Penny said, "Saw you arrive. Why you here?"

First one said, "Armed robbery, the economy is shit, you know."

"Kidnapping, my own kid. Domestic. Took him away from his no good mother," said the second.

"That sucks," Bad Penny said, "arrested for doing the right thing."

"Tell me about it," the man agreed.

***

Bad Penny kept up his routine for the next three weeks. Working out everyday and continuing to put on muscle due to the massive amounts of beef and the occasional chicken they forced him to eat when they ran short of beef.

"Hey asshole," he said to a guard, "can't you get these sons-of-bitches to quit jacking off? I'm tired of listening to these motherfuckers and their goddamn moaning." One morning the guy in the cell directly across from him, a goddamn Mexican, stood up, dropped his pants and facing Bad Penny, started stroking himself. Bad Penny didn't want to be the object of any man's fantasies. "Fuck, couldn't you at least wait til after breakfast? No? Aiight then," he said to the latino con, "next time we're out of these cells I'm going to kick your fucking, queer ass."

Bad Penny was growing worse by the day. More foul mouthed and short tempered by the minute.

The week of Bad Penny's execution arrived.

"You know this is my last week in this shithole," he said to the server dishing up the meat for breakfast. "They're gettin' ready to stick a fucking needle in my white ass. I hope I can have all the goddamn burgers I want this week."

"Well, you're in luck, asshole."

Monday, Tuesday and for his first two meals Wednesday Bad Penny had all the hamburgers he wanted, doubles, with chili, cheese and everything else.

At dinner Wednesday, Bad Penny went with all the other cons on his cell block to dinner. The server, as usual, put his three hamburgers on a tray and handed it to him. His last meal before his execution Thursday morning.

Pennington Wentworth, II pushed his tray along the shiny silver rails, a queasy feeling forming in his stomach, and turning back to the server, he gently, sweetly, said, "Excuse me, my dear man, but I don't eat red meat. Is there any way I could get a nice salad?"

www.ingramcontent.com/pod-product-compliance
Lightning Source LLC
Chambersburg PA
CBHW020136180626
46810CB00004B/1587